"Mama!"

"What in the world are you doing here!" Geraldine's rage had boiled over.

The people in the lobby were all ears. All eyes.

Geraldine grabbed Doris by the hand. Doris pulled away.

"Mama, please, you're embarrassing me."

"*I'm* embarrassing *you*!"

Doris cringed at the sight of all the people in the lobby. Gawking. Murmuring. Snickering.

"Look at you all gussied up like some woman twice your age with half your sense? And in a place like this!" her mother cried out.

"But, Mama, I want to be a singer, a real singer, and this is where I have to be if I'm going to learn anything."

"Girl! Don't you know that road is paved with nothing but temptations?"

"But, but, Mama, I want to sing," Doris whimpered as Geraldine yanked her through the lobby and out the doors of the Apollo Theatre.

Other Point books you will enjoy:

The Party's Over
by Caroline B. Cooney

Tell Me How the Wind Sounds
by Leslie Davis Guccione

Winter Dreams, Christmas Love
by Mary Francis Shura

MAMA, I WANT TO SING

Vy Higginsen with Tonya Bolden

SCHOLASTIC INC.
New York Toronto London Auckland Sydney

The authors gratefully acknowledge the following copyright holders for their permission to reprint the material specified below:

"This Bitter Earth" by Clyde Otis. Copyright © 1959, 1960 by Alley Music Corp., Trio Music Co., Inc., and IZA Music Corp. Copyright renewed. Used by permission. All rights reserved.

"God Bless the Child" by Arthur Herzog, Jr., and Billie Holiday. Copyright © 1941 by Edward B. Marks Music Company. Copyright renewed. Used by permission. All rights reserved.

"This Little Light of Mine" by Lillian Bowles, Charles Pace, copyright © 1934 (renewed) UNICHAPPEL MUSIC, INC. All rights reserved. Used by permission.

"We've Come This Far by Faith" by Albert A. Goodson. Copyright © 1963 by Manna Music, Inc., 25510 Avenue Stanford, Suite 101, Valencia, CA 91355. International Copyright secured. All rights reserved. Used by permission.

"In My Solitude" by Irvin Mills, Duke Ellington, and Eddie De Lange. Copyright © 1934 by Mills Music, Inc. Copyright renewed © 1962 by Mills Music, Inc. and Scarsdale Music Corp. International Copyright secured. Made in USA. All rights reserved.

ISBN 0-590-44202-3

12 11 10 9 8 7 6 5 4 3 2   4 5 6 7/9

This book is dedicated to those people nearest and dearest to my heart — my family:

> *My Inspiring Mother, Geraldine*
> *My Husband and Creative Partner, Ken Wydro*
> *My Loving Daughter, Knoelle*
> *My Nephew and Business Consultant, Kery Davis, esq.*
> *My Talented Sister, Doris Troy*
> *My Wise and Steady Sister, Joyce Davis*
> *My Enthusiastic Brother, Randolph A. Higginson*

I am thankful and grateful to all cast, crew, staff, friends, and millions of audience members who made the musical Mama, I Want To Sing *a learning and a growing process — a dream and a vision come true.*

V.H.

> *In loving memory of my mother,*
> *Georgia C. Bolden, who believed in me.*

T.B.

Contents

Prologue

The bright and mighty sun stood her ground high up in the pale blue sky, but the wind was everywhere. It barreled down the Harlem streets, sweeping clean the gutters. It swirled around rooftop water tanks. It sent leaves scurrying for cover. Up and down the avenues, through side streets as well, the wind nipped at the hats of ladies, gents, and tots dodging it on their way to church.

Several miles south — and what seemed like a world away — at 10:25 A.M., Doris Winter stepped into a limousine parked in front of the Sherry Netherland Hotel at Fifth Avenue and 59th Street.

Doris Winter had arrived in New York the previous afternoon. That evening she enjoyed a quiet dinner with her mother in her hotel suite. And after dinner they had one of their typical debates.

"Doris, don't go trying to tell me what to do."

"Mama, you're being silly. It's late, it's getting chilly and, anyway, that's what the car is for."

"Doris, you know full well I can get the number two bus right over here at Madison Avenue and it puts me off right around the corner from the house. And besides, you know I hate limousines, 'specially black ones. Remind me too much of funerals."

"Well, will you take a taxi?" Doris asked.

"You know don't no yellow cab want to go up to Harlem these days."

"Mama, the doorman will see to it that you get one that'll take you anywhere you want to go. Better than that, I'll come down and personally see to it. Okay?" Meeting with no objections, Doris continued, "Okay. That's settled."

Doris helped her mother into the taxi and pressed a twenty-dollar bill into her hand. As the taxi moved away from the curb, Doris called out, "I love you. See you tomorrow." Once inside the hotel lobby she said to herself, I know. She'll tell the taxi driver to let her out at the bus stop and put the twenty in the offering plate tomorrow.

Tomorrow came quickly. Before Doris knew it, she had gone through her morning meditation, fine-tuned two of the songs she had written for her next album, breakfasted, showered, dressed, and was on her way uptown.

As the limousine made its way through Central Park, Doris looked out at the leafless trees shivering in the wind and thought about how long it had been since she had been to Mt. Calvary. A whirl of emotions raced through her, tugging at her heart. Haven't felt this nervous in a long, long time, maybe not since my first night at the Apollo, she thought. If this were Madison Square Garden, I'd be in better control. But then, this is not a performance. It's a strange thing, scary even, to come face to face with so many memories.

The limousine came out of the park and headed toward Lenox Avenue. Doris looked around Harlem with a shudder. The hollow buildings with broken windows made her sigh deeply. What a waste, she thought, what a shame.

As the limousine neared the corner of 130th Street, a fierce breeze rattled the crowd milling around the church steps. A remnant of that breeze gave Doris a nudge as she emerged from her limousine. "Oohs" and "aahs" ballooned into the air as the driver closed the car door behind her.

"There she is, Miss Emma. Can you see her good?"

"I can see her right fine," Miss Emma replied.

"Yo, Lady D., wuzzup?" a young man hooted.

"My Lord! Don't she look good," a middle-aged woman said to her friend.

"Girl, I told you her pictures don't do her no justice," the friend boasted.

Doris hadn't meant to dazzle, but she was a star. And it showed. It wasn't so much the expensive shoes, the sapphire-and-diamond earrings, or the sable coat for that matter. It was something about the way her heels clicked against the pavement; something about the way she held her head; some-

thing about the humble, yet unmistakably regal way
Doris mounted the reddish-brown steps of Mt. Calvary Full Gospel Church.

In the vestibule of the church, an usher handed
Doris a program. He was an elderly man with a face
that announced, "I'm in a bad mood and I like it
that way!" Doris thought the man looked familiar,
but she couldn't quite place him. She was trying to
do just that when she found herself pressed on every
side by people asking her to autograph their pro-
grams. As she was about to sign one for a little girl,
the usher boomed out, "Everybody stand back! Clear
the way, now! With all due respect, ladies and
gentlemen, I know you're all excited to see Miss
Winter, but let us not forget that we have gathered
here today to worship the Lord, not some superstar,
if you know what I mean."

Doris penned "Best Wishes and God Bless" on
the little girl's program and said to herself, I *knew*
that face was familiar. It's Brother Cooper! As she
entered the sanctuary she thought, Good Lord! After
all these years . . . still a grouch.

Hubbub and chitter-chatter swizzled around the
sanctuary as Doris walked up the center aisle. The
congregation followed her steps with whispers, eyes
wide with curiosity, and with clicks and flashes.
Behind her she could hear Brother Cooper shushing
people and threatening to confiscate their cameras.
When she reached the first pew on her right, Doris
smiled at the two women sitting there and sat between them. The instant she did, with a lift of his
eyebrow the Minister of Music signaled the organist
to strike the first chords of Mt. Calvary's standard

processional hymn, "We've Come This Far by Faith."

With hymnals in hand, the congregation stood and the choir began its march into the sanctuary: down the center aisle, fanning out to the right and the left, and singing:

> We've come this far by faith
> Leaning on the Lord . . .

With the passing of the blue and white robes, Doris whispered, "The choir was the source. . . . The music was the inspiration."

Doris fixed her eyes on the simple oak cross suspended above the pulpit and joined in the processional hymn with all her heart, mind, and fullness of her voice. Tears glistened in her eyes. As she sought to steady her emotions, Doris drifted into memories of one of her yesterdays, to the evening when it all began, an evening when at choir rehearsal she stepped out from the shadows of the back row.

Part One

"This Little Light of Mine"

One

It was a Wednesday evening in February 1946. Choir rehearsal at Mt. Calvary.

The Second World War, which had ruptured so many lives around the world, was over. In America, as families regathered and regrouped, the country seemed to utter one huge sigh of relief now that there was peace. But all was not right in America. For one, African Americans who had helped free others from Nazi control found that back home they were still bound by injustice. Jim Crow was sitting pretty in the South. In the North, he was living under an alias. For millions of African Americans, it was the churches that held strong as refuges from abuse and injustice, as greenhouses for dreams: churches like Harlem's majestic Abyssinian Baptist Church and the smaller, but no less dynamic ones like Mt. Calvary, eight blocks south of Abyssinian, on Lenox Avenue and 130th Street.

Doris Winter's father, Randolph A. Winter, was the pastor of Mt. Calvary, and so her life revolved around the church. Next to Sunday service, her favorite time in church was Wednesday evening when she went with her mother to choir rehearsal.

The rehearsal room was in the basement of the church. It was a large rectangular room with whitewashed concrete walls and a speckled linoleum floor that buckled and cracked in a few places. The room contained a mixed bag of things: an upright piano, a long walnut plank-top table, a rolltop desk, a large standing mirror, a few old benches, and a dozen or so ladder-back folding chairs. Toward the back of the room there were bookcases filled with Bibles, hymnals, songbooks, and sheet music. Close by were several rows of clothes racks, some with choir robes and ushers' uniforms, others with men's, women's, and children's clothing that members of Missionary Circle #4 fixed up close to brand-new and distributed to whomsoever needed a helping hand.

As usual, on that particular Wednesday evening in February 1946, Doris and her mother, Geraldine, arrived at the church well before seven o'clock. Whereas some pastors' wives spent their time grandstanding as First Lady of the Church, Geraldine spent hers doing hands-on churchwork. She had already put out the folding chairs, and was now seated at the walnut plank-top table making alterations on a few choir robes. Doris sat across from her studying her vocabulary words for this week's spelling bee.

"Antonym. Baton. Cardigan. Fahrenheit. Monument. Pyramid. Revolution. Salamander. Vertical.

Xylophone," Doris repeated softly, punctuating each word with a nod of her head. The third time around she paused on "cardigan."

"Mama, I know what kind of sweater I have on."

"What kind, baby?"

"A cardigan," Doris proudly said, adding a rapid: "*C-A-R-D-I-G-A-N*."

"That's right, baby."

"And my skirt is plaid."

"Uh-huh. And that kind of plaid is called Glen plaid," her mother said.

Doris got a little carried away and began to review her entire outfit for her mother. "My skirt is Glen plaid, my sweater is a red cardigan, my shoes are black oxfords, my tights are gray, my — "

Doris's ponytails fell just above her earlobes. They were weighted down by two large bows. Her problem right now was that she couldn't see her hair and couldn't remember the color of her bows. She dashed over to the mirror.

"My ribbons are red," she said triumphantly. Over her shoulder she asked, "Mama, what's this stuff on my collar?"

"It's called rickrack, baby."

"Rickrack," Doris snapped as she surveyed herself in the mirror. "Rick. Rack."

Doris was not as tall as she would have liked to have been. Her hair was not as long as Melinda Brooks's (the girl in her class whose best friend everyone wanted to be). And Doris hated it when grownups called her pudgy. Unfortunately, Doris sometimes spent so much time thinking about all that she wasn't and wished she were that she

couldn't see all the beautiful things about herself.
Like her bright, inquisitive eyes, and her dark coffee-
colored skin that seemed to drink up the sun even
when it wasn't shining. And then there was her voice
with its ability to ring out clear, crisp notes and glide
through the scales the way a dancer can walk up
and down a flight of familiar stairs. She was also a
great imitator with a special knack for reproducing
a sound after hearing it just once. People were
amused and moved to laughter by her sounds, her
clings and clangs, her clicks and ticks and tocks.

"Rick. Rack," Doris snapped as she turned from
the mirror and, bored with her little game of show
and tell, moved over to the piano. Ever so softly she
diddled with the keys, trying to tinkle out a tune. At
one point she grazed the ivory with her fingertips,
racing down the keyboard with a flourish, passion-
ately wriggling her fingers and imagining that she
was making glorious, thunderous music. Geraldine
soon brought her concert to a close with, "That's
enough now, Doris. Come over here and pack up
your school things. Rehearsal will be starting soon."

By six-thirty the rehearsal room was buzzing with
greetings and banter as the choir members arrived
one by one. At a quarter to seven the choir members
began assembling themselves in their places.
Doris's place was at the end of the back row because
Geraldine never let Doris too far out of her sight.
There Doris sang along with the choir, often getting
so carried away that she sang louder than she
realized.

Before the clock chimed seven times, a hush fell

over the rehearsal room. Byron Wesley, the Minister of Music, had arrived.

Byron Wesley had been born with an ear and a heart for music. When he was ten years old and living in Decatur, Georgia, his grandmother had taken him to a Roland Hayes concert in nearby Atlanta. Byron was spellbound by the internationally renowned tenor: he marveled at all the different kinds of songs he sang. He became even more taken with the man when his grandmother leaned over during the concert and whispered, "You know, Byron, Roland Hayes once gave a command performance before King George the Fifth at Buckingham Palace." By the end of the evening Byron had found his idol.

Although he never became as famous as Roland Hayes, he did achieve great acclaim in Harlem and on the church choir circuit in the Northeast, as a singer, choir director, composer, and teacher of voice and piano. As his grandmother always used to say, "World-famous or not, a hero is still a hero; a success, still a success."

At 5′8″ and 153 pounds, Byron Wesley was certainly not a large man, but he had an air about him that made people treat him with the utmost respect. He was as precise and meticulous about his appearance as he was about music. Never a fleck of lint on his shoulder, a gravy stain on his tie, or a crease on his trousers. And tucked in his vest pocket, his gold pocket watch was certain to have the correct time — down to the second.

Doris was particularly enchanted by his hands:

soft, smooth, and not a mark or scar anywhere. Whenever she looked into his face she couldn't help thinking of a fox, a stern but friendly fox whose manner and movements fascinated her. She was also intrigued by the way he sometimes talked about music, especially the little speech she often heard him give a new choir member: "I will require more than raw talent. . . . I will expect punctuality. Reverence for music. A quiet mind. An open mind. A willingness to practice with passion and listen to the voice within in pursuit of that most exquisite of things: Excellence."

So uncompromising was the Minister of Music on the issue of excellence that rumor had it he would make his choir practice, practice, and practice one and the same song until singers' knees buckled, eyes watered, necks stretched. They practiced until they got it — not right — but perfect: perfect breathing, perfect harmony, perfect pitch, and perfect control.

"Breathing, harmony, pitch, control. Breathing, harmony, pitch, control. Breathing, harmony, pitch, control," said the Minister of Music as he made his way in front of the choir.

As always, choir rehearsal began with a moment of silence.

"Let us be still," said the Minister of Music. "Let us turn our attentions away from our worries and concerns, from all the negative things, people, and conditions outside. Let us turn inward to connect with the source, the living God, and let us feel the power, the peace, and the energy of the love in our hearts."

During the moment of silence, Doris saw her hands gliding down a piano and prayed she would one day really be able to play.

The Minister of Music capped off the silence with a gentle, "Amen," and followed it up with a vigorous, "Now, choir, let us say 'Praise the Lord!' "

"Praise the Lord," obeyed the choir a tad limply, as thoughts of their long day at work and a worry or two crept back into their minds. But such thoughts skedaddled when the Minister of Music inquired, "Do you or do you not know that the Lord God Almighty is worthy to be praised?"

"I know. . . . Yes, ha' mercy. . . . Amen. . . . I's a witness. . . . " and other such responses sprinkled through the air.

"Well, then, once again! Let us say 'Praise the Lord!' "

The choir let out a reverberating, "Praise the Lord!" and the Minister of Music smiled, punctuating his smile with a hearty, "AMEN!" The choir let out a relaxed sigh that fluttered through the rehearsal room with perfect breathing, perfect harmony, perfect pitch, and perfect control.

"Now, choir, the first song we will rehearse tonight is 'Guide Me, O Thou Great Jehovah.' " The Minister of Music raised his eyebrow, and Sister Morgan's fingers danced down the piano.

"Now all together, for the introductory 'Bread of Heaven,' " said the Minister of Music.

The choir stretched for breathing, harmony, pitch, and control. To the average listener the choir would have sounded quite good. But for the Minister of Music "quite good" was never good enough.

"Uh-uh. Uh-uh," he thundered. "No, no, no, no, nooooo. *That* will never do. Looks like what we are going to have to do is break this song down in order to build it up again. Sopranos, I'm going to begin with you."

The Minister of Music plied the correct sound out of each section. First the sopranos, then the altos, then the tenors, then the baritones. Tenors, altos, baritones, sopranos. Baritones, tenors, sopranos, altos. Altos, sopranos, baritones, tenors. Sopranos, baritones, tenors, altos.

Doris remained silent during the exercise. She couldn't believe her ears: the voices became not only louder, but stronger, more beautiful. She couldn't believe her eyes either: She could almost see the energy, the power that leapt from the Minister of Music's hands as he pointed to each section of the choir.

Wow! Doris said to herself. How much longer is he gonna make them do this?

By this one exercise, the Minister of Music changed the whole mood and vibration of the choir. Instead of a group of individuals, the choir was now a unified whole. On the count of four they launched the song to Heaven:

> *Guide me, O Thou great Jehovah,*
> *Pilgrim thro' this barren land,*
> *I am weak, but Thou art mighty,*
> *Hold me with Thy powerful hand.*
> *Bread of Heaven,*
> *Feed me till I want no more;*

> *Bread of Heaven,*
> *Feed me till I want no more.*

Midway through the song Doris joined in, holding the notes just as long as the others. The Minister of Music took notice.

When the Minister of Music was satisfied that every verse had most definitely made it to Heaven, he brought the song to a close. On the closing note he looked up as if he were truly beholding manna falling from on high and said, "Oh, yes, yes, yes, yes, yessss! Thank you, God! *That* is the way the Mt. Calvary Inspirational Choir *ought* to sound! And speaking of sounds . . ." he continued as his eyes traveled to the back row, "Doris, would you kindly step forward."

Wide-eyed and in absolute shock, Doris began to make her way forward.

"Your voice is developing beautifully, my dear," said the Minister of Music. "And I think it would be a benefit to you as well as to all of us if you were to join the adult choir. As a matter of fact, I think you should make your debut this Sunday." Turning to Geraldine he added: "That is, Sister Winter, if it is all right with you."

Doris stopped dead in her tracks.

"By all means, Brother Wesley. I think it's fine," Geraldine Winter said.

Doris began moving forward again.

"All right now, choir," said the Minister of Music, "let us all say 'Amen' for having Doris Winter in the adult choir."

At first, the "Amen" of approval seemed unanimous. But even though he could barely see him out of the corner of his eye, the Minister of Music felt Brother Cooper's silent groan.

"Brother Cooper, is there some problem?"

Doris stood stock-still again. In unison all eyes rolled in Brother Cooper's direction.

"Well, Brother Wesley, honorable Minister of Music, with all due respect, the age requirement to be in the choir — that is, the *adult* choir — is seventeen, if you know what I mean."

"*And*, Brother Cooper?" said the Minister of Music with nostrils flaring.

"Well, Doris is only, what, nine or — "

"She turned eleven last month," Geraldine snapped.

"Well, same difference," Brother Cooper snapped back. "Anyway, as I was saying, Brother Wesley, honorable Minister of Music, in this humble Christian soldier's opinion, speaking of myself, if you understand, just because she is the pastor's daughter is no reason — "

"Brother Jacob Ezekiel Cooper!" the Minister of Music interrupted. "I rebuke that jealous and contentious spirit in the name of Jesus! That attitude, sir, has got to be changed. You need to go to the altar and on bended knee ask the Lord to help you. Because, you see, Brother Cooper, it does not matter how big or how important or how *anything* you may think you are in this life, you are still a pilgrim."

All eyes were now fixed on the Minister of Music.

"Doris Winter is joining because she has a talent. A talent is a talent is a talent! No matter how old it is or in whose body it is. This child can sing, and

I would want her in the adult choir no matter whose daughter she was. Is that clear, Brother Cooper?"

"Yes, sir."

"May we continue our rehearsal?"

"Yes, sir."

"Doris, my dear, come here. Stand with the sopranos, please, right next to your mother." With Doris in position he continued, "That's good. . . . Now, once again, choir, let us say 'Amen' for having Doris Winter in the choir."

The choir said "Amen" and "Amen" and "Amen." Loudly. Clearly. With conviction.

"All right, choir," said the Minister of Music, "one more time. On the count of four, let's hear how Mt. Calvary can sound."

With a lift of his eyebrow and a flourish of his hands the Minister of Music signaled the choir to sing the first verse of the song that was by now permanently impressed on their vocal cords. As the singing continued, Brother Cooper repented of his jealous and contentious spirit. And under the tender gaze of her mother, and the Minister of Music's encouraging nods, Doris settled in as a member of the choir.

The choir rehearsed three more songs that evening, the last of which was their signature song, "Travelin' Shoes." Whenever the choir gave concerts at other churches someone almost always made a special request for "Travelin' Shoes." It was an upbeat, bouncy song full of soul-stirring rhythms. Every time the choir performed the song they brought the house down — or, as the churchfolk would say, they "tore the house up." Tore the anger and backbiting out of peoples' hearts, tore the fears, pains, and despair from their souls, and in their places planted love, joy, and peace.

As it usually did, that night during choir rehearsal the song took on a life of its own. It built to a feverish pitch that sent Sister Grier diving into her shopping bag for her tambourine, and Brother Calloway scrambling for a pair of blocks to clack, clack, clack to the beat. Sister Morgan worked the piano as if she had four hands. Others turned their feet and hands into instruments of music, instruments of the Lord.

They were having a high time in the basement of Mt. Calvary Full Gospel Church. The Minister of Music was the first to break out into a shout. He moved from side to side, jumped up and down straight as an arrow, hopped on one foot, then on the other. With his knees bent, his back at a forty-five-degree angle, and his palms facing out, he raised his arms from his sides like an eagle taking flight. He spun around fast enough to make the Devil dizzy. And whatever move the Minister of Music made, he was always moving to the beat.

When the spirit hit the alto section of the choir some hands went flailing in the air. Tears of joy streamed down the faces of others. One woman thrust both arms up in the air, shook her head from side to side, and proclaimed, "Praise the Lord! Praise the Lord!"

Hallelujahs were everywhere.

Doris was singing her heart out, totally lost in the music, the voices, and the rhythms that told her hands how to clap, her feet how to stamp, her body how to rear back and let loose the notes welling up from her soul.

As the churchfolk say, "The Holy Spirit don't make a fool out of nobody." This being the case, at quarter to ten the Holy Spirit let everybody know that it was getting late and time to start heading home. When the last "hallelujah" had been uttered, just as it had begun so choir rehearsal ended with a moment of silence.

The Minister of Music broke the silence with, "Oh, God Almighty, we thank you for the gift of song and thy sweet, sweet, sweet inspiration. Amen."

The choir members soon began leaving in pairs and groups of threes. Before he exited the room the Minister of Music walked over to Doris, shook her hand, and said, "My dear, welcome to the adult choir."

"Doris, do you realize what an honor Brother Wesley bestowed upon you tonight?" Geraldine said after everyone had gone.

"Oh, yes, Mama!" Doris nodded rapidly.

Geraldine snuggled Doris up in a big hug and planted a kiss on her forehead. "Baby girl, I'm so proud of you," she added as they rocked from side to side. "But that reminds me, I better see about getting you a robe of your own, little lady."

While Geraldine searched through the racks for the smallest robe, Doris sat back on one of the benches with her hands under her thighs, palms flat against the seat, swinging her legs in and out, in and out, and softly humming "Travelin' Shoes."

After a few minutes Doris said to herself with glee, I'm going to be in the adult choir. Soon she turned

the sentence into a singsong chant. Instinctively she
started to add the refrain "na, na, na, na, na." Then
she remembered that wasn't a nice thing to do.
Instead she made the refrain "rickrack, rickrack."

"I'm going to be in the adult choir. Rickrack,
rick — " Doris broke off and raced over to her
mother.

"Mama! Wait till we tell Daddy!"

Two

All the way home Doris thought about how she was going to tell her father her big news. She was hardly through the front door when she yelled out, "Daddy!"

"In here, pumpkin," Reverend Winter called out from his study in a deep, resonant voice that suited the large bear of a man that he was. When he heard Doris clattering up the stairs, he shifted in his armchair and laid his book on the side table.

Doris bounded through the doorway with, "Daddy! Guess what?"

"Wait a minute there. How about a 'Good evening' and a 'How do you do?' "

"GoodeveningandhowdoyoudoDaddy, but, Daddy, guess what?"

"I can't begin to guess what could have you stirred up so."

"Come on, Daddy, guess!"

"Let's see. . . . You received an *A* on your book report."

"No, guess again."

"You won first place in the spelling bee."

"*Daddy,* spelling bees are on Fridays."

"Oh, my dear, why, of course. I beg your pardon," Reverend Winter said with mock humility and a playful bow.

"Come on, Daddy, guess again."

"Doris, I must confess you have me stumped." Pointing to his book he added, "And here I thought Mueller's exegesis on St. Paul's epistles to the Corinthians was a challenge."

"Huh?"

"What I'm saying, pumpkin, is, I give up."

"Tonight at choir rehearsal I was singing along like I always do and Brother Wesley heard me and he told me I was good and then he said that if it was all right with Mama I could be in the adult choir and I could sing on Sunday."

"A solo?"

"Well, we might have a ways to go before we get to that," said Geraldine, who stood in the doorway smiling in on the scene. "But she will be singing with the choir on Sunday. And that reminds me, I want to get started on her robe tonight." As Geraldine left the doorway, Reverend Winter lifted Doris onto his lap.

"So my little girl is in the adult choir! Well, glory be to God!" After a hug he added, "Tell you what. After service on Sunday, how about you and me and Mama go out to the Chinese restaurant for dinner to celebrate."

"Can I have moo goo gai pan and extra fortune cookies?"

"You can have anything you like."

Thirty minutes later Doris lay in her bed still full of excitement and fighting sleep. As she drifted toward dreamland, she thought, Oh, boy, I can't wait to tell Toni.

Toni's full name was Antoinette Kollontai Sojourner Dunmore Barnett, and she took great pride in her string of names. Many of her schoolmates thought Toni a bit strange. For behind her doe eyes whirled a mind as sharp as a tack and an imagination that went off like fireworks at the oddest times. Put the two together and what the teachers had on their hands was an *A*-student who talked out of turn and sidetracked lessons with a thousand and one questions. Toni constantly bombarded her fellow students with her knowledge. And because she wasn't soft-spoken when she turned to one student at the lunch table with an avalanche of "Did you know's?" the entire table had to be educated and enlightened.

Very often, Toni sat alone at lunchtime.

Doris didn't find Toni so strange. Moreover, she was fascinated by all the things Toni knew. Also, Toni accepted Doris. Whereas some of her schoolmates sometimes ridiculed Doris because, as the most obnoxious put it, her father was a "preacher-preacher man," Toni wasn't bothered and was even a little intrigued. In fact, had Doris's father not been a minister, Toni and Doris might never have become friends in the first place.

"Hi, Doris," Toni had said one day in the school cafeteria.

"Hi, Toni," Doris responded hesitantly as Toni took a seat next to her and the students seated around Doris fled to another table.

"Your father's a minister, right?"

"Yes," Doris replied a little defensively.

"Good! You're just the person I want to talk to. You see, last night Professor Foster was at the house and he was telling my parents that Moses's wife was an African woman. I was just wondering if you could ask your father if that's true."

"I could ask him, or you could maybe ask your Sunday school teacher."

"Oh, I don't go to church."

"*Never?*" Doris said.

"When I visit my grandmother in Boston, she makes me go sometimes. Boy, is that boring! A lot of the service is in Latin."

"Is that like pig Latin?" Doris asked.

"What's pig Latin?"

"You know, what grown-ups talk sometimes when they don't want kids to know what they're saying. Like . . . like, er-hay esent-pray is-yay in-yay uh-thay oset-clay. That means, 'Her present is in the closet.' "

"No, I'm talking about the Latin they used to speak in ancient Rome. My father said I should study it one day because it'll be good training for my mind. I guess, if nothing else, at least I'll understand what goes on at my grandmother's church. But I'll probably still fall asleep," Toni said.

"Sometimes I fall asleep during the announcements, but most of the time I'm wide awake. Nothing boring about our church. And the best part is the singing and the music. It makes you clap and smile and sometimes want to — "

"Maybe I could come to church with you one day?" Toni asked.

"That'd be fun."

"And they don't speak Latin in your church, right?"

"No. But people speak in tongues sometimes when — "

"What's *that?*" Toni interrupted.

Before long, Doris and Toni were eating lunch together almost every day. Doris talked a lot about the church. Toni talked about the little she knew or thought she knew about everything under the sun.

As Doris and Toni were walking home from school the day after Doris became a member of the adult choir, Doris shared her news with Toni almost as excitedly as she had shared it with her father the night before. Toni listened with eager ears.

The two looked the classic odd couple. Doris with her tweed overcoat buttoned to the neck and her burgundy hat and scarf exactly as Geraldine had fixed them on her that morning. Her galoshes were properly fastened and protecting her oxfords underneath, the laces of which were still double-knotted. Doris's mittened hands hugged her book-bag to her chest.

Toni's navy blue sailor's cap was cocked back on her head, her peacoat was unbuttoned from the waist up, and her right sock sagged around her calf muscle. Every few steps a bit of slush slipped into her loafers, one of which was minus a penny. Her

bookbag was slung over her left shoulder and went
bump-bump against her back.

"Usually you have to be in the junior choir first
and then when you're older you can try out for the
adult choir," Doris informed Toni as they neared
the corner of 128th Street and Fifth Avenue. "And
you know what else?"

"What else?" Toni asked.

"I get to sing this Sunday, and this Sunday is first
Sunday — "

"Why's that special?"

"It's the biggest Sunday of the month. It's when
we have communion and — "

"What's that again?" Toni interrupted yet again.

"It's when we remember what Jesus did for us,
how he died for our sins. Then you eat a wafer that
tastes like paper and you drink some grape juice
out of a tiny cup that looks sorta like a big thimble.
. . . Before you do all that, though, you have to
search your heart and get rid of all the bad feelings,
like if you're mad at somebody. And you're 'sposed
to tell God you're sorry for everything you did
wrong."

"In your whole life?"

"No. Just since the last time you took communion," Doris answered.

"That can't be that bad. . . . But what if you forget
something you did wrong?"

"Well, you just tell God you're sorry even for the
things you don't remember. Just to be safe, a lot of
times I tell God I'm sorry for the wrong stuff I did
that maybe I didn't know was wrong."

"That makes sense."

"I think so, too," Doris said as she stepped off the curb. "Well, see you tomorrow."

"I'll walk you to Lenox."

When Doris and Toni reached the other side of Fifth Avenue, Toni picked up their conversation. "So, are you nervous about Sunday morning?"

"What's there to be nervous about? I know all the songs real good and I know everybody at church and — "

"Does this mean you'll become a professional singer?"

"A *professional* singer?" Doris asked with surprise.

"Yeah! You're not gonna just sing in the church choir your whole life?"

"What's wrong with that?"

"Nothing's *wrong* with it," Toni replied. "It's just that you should, well, broaden your horizons. Like my father's always saying, 'We Negroes are never going to improve our station in life until we broaden our horizons.' So that's my advice to you, Doris. Broaden your horizons. You can always sing in the church choir. What about singing for the whole wide world? Now *that's* something to think about!"

"Oh, Toni, I could never sing for the whole wide — "

"I can see it now," exclaimed Toni, her imagination off and running. "You'll be at the Apollo, then the Savoy. . . . Next stop, Paris, France. I can see you now on the steps of the Palais de something in a long satin evening gown and a chinchilla coat!

with a ten-foot train. . . . Long strands of pearls around your neck, diamonds on your fingers, dozens of long-stemmed roses in your hands . . . posing for photographers. You'll be more famous than Josephine Baker. Of course, you'll have to change your name. That's what a lot of people do, you know. How about Gabriella Lolita? Or Michelle La-Montague? Or . . . I got it! Dorissa . . . what's your middle name?"

"Oh, Toni!"

"I mean it. I think you should become a world-famous singer. Yep. A world-famous singer. And we can send each other postcards from around the world."

"What are you talking about?"

"Well, I'm going to be a writer and travel all around — "

"A writer? I thought you were going to be a — "

"An astronomer? Not anymore. I'm going to be a writer now. Like Langston Hughes, or Countee Cullen, or Alice Dunbar-Nelson, or . . ."

As Toni rattled off a string of names, many of which Doris had never heard of, Doris found herself infected by Toni's imagination. She lit up on the inside and began to smile as she wondered what it would be like to be a world-famous singer, or just a famous singer in America, or just a singer in New York. As her wondering grew narrower and narrower, Doris couldn't imagine anything except singing in Mt. Calvary's Inspirational Choir.

By now, Doris and Toni had reached Lenox Avenue. They split up. Toni headed one block north and back over to Fifth Avenue; Doris, two blocks south to 126th Street.

At the dinner table that evening, out of the blue, Doris asked, "Mama. Daddy. Do you think I could be a singer when I grow up? You know a, uh, professional singer, almost sorta like Sister Carrie used to be?"

"You mean out in the world?" Geraldine frowned.

"Geraldine, let the child dream a little," Reverend Winter said gently but firmly. And, as he caught the flicker of a dream spark up again in Doris's eyes, he added, "A little dreaming is good for the soul, and you never can tell how dreams are going to turn out. You know, when I was back home in Barbados and only a little older than you, Doris, I began to have a dream of becoming a preacher. Friday night prayer meetings at Glory Hill Tabernacle were glorious times indeed. As if lifted by a wind, I found myself standing before the congregation interpreting Scripture and preaching the Word with a fierceness that was not my own. It was as if there was an older, wiser person deep down inside of me."

Doris looked deep into her father's eyes and tried hard to see him as a boy.

"Soon I started to dream of becoming a preacher, and maybe having a little church of my own in Barbados. But little did I know that my pastor would take me under his wing and help me get a scholarship to a seminary in the States. And lo and behold, here I come to pastor a church in Harlem."

"I know, Daddy," Doris sighed. "And one day you

were walking down Lenox Avenue and you saw a boarded-up church and a still, small voice said, 'This is it.' "

"That's right, pumpkin, and — "

"And another voice said, 'That's a mighty big church and you don't even have a single church member.' But you listened to the still, small voice, right, Daddy?"

"Are you trying to tell me you're tired of my storytelling, Doris?"

"No, it's not that. It's just that I want you to get to the good part. You know, skip the part about how hard you worked, and the Depression, and how you slept on a cot in the back of the church, and how you only had one suit and two good shirts, and you walked everywhere to save car fare, and how God blessed you with the job at the post office at a time when Negroes didn't get those kinds of jobs."

"Okay, little Miss Impatient, let's see. . . ." Reverend Winter said with a smile. "You mean the day Sister Beard brought a visitor to Mt. Calvary?"

"Yeah, that's the good part!"

"Ah, yes. . . . I can remember as if it were yesterday. When the time came for us to welcome visitors, a young woman with coal-black wavy hair stood up and said, 'My name is Geraldine Payne and I bring you greetings from Briar Street Baptist Church in West Point, Virginia."

"And then . . . ?" Doris urged him on.

"And then, I felt a flutter in my chest, and all through service my eyes kept landing on that caramel beauty from West Point, Virginia, who had a smile that sent out rays of loving-kindness. . . ."

"Oooh, Mama, you were smiling at Daddy during church service."

"I was not, I was smiling at his preaching is all," Geraldine insisted.

"Well, you were sure smiling at me when I invited you and Sister Beard out for ice cream that afternoon."

"Oh, Randy, stop it!"

Doris loved it when her mother called her father "Randy." Most of the time she called him "Rev" like everybody else, and Doris knew that when she said "Randy," she was feeling extra-special feelings for him.

"And then you got married?" Doris said.

"Not right away," said Geraldine, "but that night I did write home asking my folks if I could stay up North a little while longer. A few weeks later I wrote and told them I had found a job and wanted to give New York a longer look."

"And while your Mama was, as she puts it, giving New York another look, I was eyeing a certain brownstone on 126th Street," Reverend Winter continued.

"I know," Doris said, "and you worked harder and harder, and you worked overtime and double shifts, and when you bought it, in the beginning you had a lot of tenants and you lived in one room and you still slept on a cot and still only had one good suit."

"Right again," said Reverend Winter, a tad exasperated that Doris was again rushing him to get to the good part. "And about a year after that is when we got married." Reverend Winter reached out for Geraldine's hand and added, "And in your

mother I found a gold mine. . . . And the Lord blessed
us mightily. And do you know what was the most
blessed event of all?"

"What?" Doris asked eagerly.

"The day you were born."

"And when your father first held you in his arms,"
said Geraldine softly, "he cried and cried and cried."

"That's right," Reverend Winter admitted, "and I
wasn't ashamed of tear one, because I had never
seen anything so beautiful in my whole life. You
were a dream come true. And the day we brought
you home I started focusing even harder on my
dream of making this house a real home for you
and your mother. Pretty soon, your mama had the
'proper' parlor and dining room she always wanted
down here, and on the second floor we had our
bedroom, a study for me, and a bedroom for you.
And now that we have no tenants at all, we'll have
two nice guest rooms on the third floor and, Lord
willing, I'm going to turn downstairs into a huge
recreation room. . . . So you see, pumpkin, everything I am, and everything I have, started with a
dream. And that's why I say go ahead and dream."
With a quick glance over at Geraldine he added,
"Just make sure you let the Lord direct the path your
dreaming should follow."

Three

Two days later Reverend Winter was again thinking about his dreams for his family as he walked around Harlem, replaying in his mind a conversation he'd had that afternoon with his friend and Senior Usher Board Member, Dr. Gus Fleming.

"I don't like what I see, Rev," said Dr. Fleming after a routine physical checkup. "Your blood pressure is up. You have dark circles under your eyes. Any chest pains or shortness of breath?"

"Not really. Well, sometimes. When I'm walking up stairs or lifting something heavy. I may get a little dizzy, or feel a little tightness, but nothing sharp or — "

As he went on to downplay his symptoms, Dr. Fleming listened patiently. Then he told Reverend Winter he wanted him to check into Harlem Hospital first thing Monday morning so he could run a few tests. "And Rev . . ." Dr. Fleming concluded, "I don't

want you to preach tomorrow. I know how you get
all riled up and — "

"But, Gus, you know tomorrow's first Sunday."

"Rev, the congregation has known and will continue to know many more first Sundays, but they
will only know one you. Now, part of the assistant
pastor's job is to take the pastor's place sometimes,
right? So when you get home, call up Reverend
Grady and — "

"But, Gus — "

"Rev, listen to me. You need to slow down. I mean
it. If you want to watch Doris grow up and see her
get married, and bounce a grandchild or two on
your knee, you've got to start taking better care of
yourself. Think about it."

Reverend Winter did just that as he walked the
streets of Harlem. As the pale winter sun went down
and the temperature dropped, he headed home.
When he arrived he told Doris and Geraldine to go
ahead with dinner without him.

"I'll catch a bite to eat a little later. Haven't got
my sermon yet," he said as he headed up to his
study.

The study was unusually still. It was as if the large
oak desk, the bookshelves, the armchair, and even
the oriental rug were holding their breath. Reverend
Winter sat down at his desk, and reached into the
bottom drawer for his old shoe box where he kept
his bankbook, the mortgage contract, the house and
life insurance policies. As he reviewed each item,
his heart grew heavy and his spirits sank: there was
less insurance money than he thought, more blank
pages in the bankbook than he had remembered.

Yes, the mortgage on the house was paid up to date, but there were still another six or seven years of payments to go. Over the years as his congregation increased, so had the freewill pastor's offering collected every Sunday. Members of his congregation were generous, but few were wealthy. If he had to go to the hospital for something serious, if he could not work . . . how could his family live?

Reverend Winter took a deep breath and banished these thoughts from his mind.

To preach or not to preach? That was the real question. And with that thought, Reverend Winter reached for his Bible, closed his eyes, and whispered, "Guide me, dear Lord Jesus." He sat for a moment in total silence. Then, with eyes still closed, he opened the Bible and let his hands lie on the pages. "Show me the way, dear God. Tell me what to do."

When he looked down, he saw that he was in the book of Ephesians. His eyes rested on Chapter 4, verse 1:

I THEREFORE, THE PRISONER OF THE LORD, BESEECH YOU THAT YE WALK WORTHY OF THE VOCATION WHEREWITH YE ARE CALLED.

Reverend Winter took this as the answer to his prayer. "Walk worthy of the vocation wherewith ye are called," he whispered.

He *would* preach tomorrow and this passage, Ephesians 4:1, would be the text for his sermon. He'd check into Harlem Hospital on Monday as Dr. Fleming had prescribed, but he was sure he could get through one more day, one more sermon.

Later that night as Reverend Winter lay in bed,

the thought he had earlier banished from his mind returned. What would happen to his family if he fell ill or . . . ? He looked over at Geraldine lying peacefully asleep. He eased out of bed, down the hall, and peeked into Doris's room where she, too, was fast asleep under a quilt Geraldine had made. The wind was rattling the window, allowing shafts of cold air to blow into his child's bedroom. He made a mental note to fix this soon. As he looked again at Doris he thought: If I were to die, what would Doris have to remember me by? What could I give her that would mean something?

Reverend Winter walked down the stairs and into the parlor. He paced the floor for a bit and then did something he had not done in a long while: he sat down at the piano. When he began to play, almost immediately, words and music began to flow before him. A picture of Doris playing on the front stoop floated across his mind. As he held the picture clear and firm in his mind, tears came to his eyes.

Upstairs, Doris was dreaming. It was like a slide show of separate but somehow related images: the Minister of Music smiling; Mama with tears in her eyes; a slender young woman in a shimmering purple dress looking out into a sea of smiling, friendly faces; lights, thunder . . . or was it applause?

The music drifted into Doris's dream and gingerly roused her from sleep. As her eyes fluttered open, the image of the woman in the purple dress leapt across her mind. Then the music lapped around and around in her head until it brought her to the light that streamed in under her bedroom door.

Reverend Winter stopped playing when he felt

eyes on his back. He turned around and found Doris standing in the archway, clutching her teddy bear, Jumpsy, in her right arm. With sleep still tickling her eyes she moved to her father's side.

"Daddy, what are you doing?"

"I'm writing a song, honey. I need some help. Please, get your composition book and something to write with. I can't write and play at the same time."

Doris ran up the flight of stairs as quietly and quickly as she could. When she couldn't find her composition book, she got mad and scared. Finally, she spied it on her bookshelf. She grabbed a pencil and scampered back downstairs.

"Okay, okay, Daddy, I'm ready," said Doris as she grabbed a small pillow from the couch and knelt down beside the piano.

"You are my child, my firstborn child," said Reverend Winter. Doris just looked at him.

"Those are the words, Doris," he said gently. "This song is for you, from me." Then he repeated the words and Doris began writing:

> *You are my child,*
> *My firstborn child.*
> *In you I see*
> *The gift of song.*

> *To keep you strong*
> *When things go wrong,*
> *To you I give this song.*
> *Follow the dream*
> *Within your heart.*

Be not afraid,
The dream's the start.

Just have the faith
To dream your dream,
Just be yourself
And dream . . .

You are my child,
My little girl.

Doris was writing as fast as she could. She wanted
her daddy to slow down. As if he could read her
mind, Reverend Winter stopped singing, but continued to play.

"How are you doing? Am I going too fast?"

"A little, Daddy. Just slow down a little, please."

Reverend Winter repeated the first two verses so
Doris could get down every word, and then he
continued.

When Reverend Winter finished the song, Doris
looked up and saw tears running down his face.
She jumped up and threw her arms around his neck.
She squeezed him as hard as she could.

"Oh, Daddy, Daddy, I love you. . . . Why are you
crying, Daddy?"

"Sometimes people cry because they are happy.
And I'm very, very happy that I have you for a daughter, Doris. I love you one hundred percent."

They hugged in silence for a long minute. Then
Reverend Winter looked deep into his daughter's
eyes.

"You've got to catch those songs when they come,

Doris. Songs have a mind of their own, you know. Remember that. Time may come when you'll be writing your own songs. . . . You've got the gift, child."

Doris heard his words, but saw something else in his eyes. Something that he was *not* saying. Doris was overcome by a strange feeling. She suddenly wanted to ask her father a lot of questions. She wanted to tell him things, too.

"Daddy . . ."

"We better get to bed now, pumpkin. Have to get up early tomorrow for church, you know," Reverend Winter said in a voice that sounded more like the daddy Doris knew.

As they headed from the parlor, Doris held Jumpsy and her composition book in one hand and slipped her other hand into her father's. "Carry me upstairs, Daddy."

"You're too big, Doris. I'm tired tonight."

"Please, Daddy, please! Just one more time."

Reverend Winter picked her up and began climbing the flight of fourteen steps to the second floor. Doris put her head on her father's shoulder as he walked slowly and with effort. "You're getting to be a big girl. Heavy, too."

At about the seventh step, Reverend Winter felt a stab of pain under his left armpit. By the time they reached the top step, he was out of breath.

Doris slid from his arms. "Daddy could you tuck me in, please."

Reverend Winter took a couple of long deep breaths and then followed Doris — composition book clutched over her heart — into her room.

"How about your prayers?" Reverend Winter asked as Doris climbed into bed.

"I said them already, but I'll say them again if you want me to." Cheerfully Doris got down on her knees. "Now I lay me down to sleep. I pray the Lord my soul to keep. If I should die before I wake, I pray the Lord my soul to take. God bless Mama, God bless Daddy, God bless Mt. Calvary. God bless everybody." After a short pause, she added: "And God, please help me sing real good tomorrow."

Reverend Winter tucked Doris in and kissed her good night. "Sweet dreams, pumpkin."

" 'Night, Daddy."

As Reverend Winter moved from the room, Doris whispered out, "I love you, Daddy. I love you one hundred percent."

Four

Before Doris knew it, Sunday morning sun was beaming into her bedroom. She scooted out of bed extra-eager to get ready for church. After all, today she was going to sing in the adult choir.

At breakfast Doris asked her mother if she could pick out something else to wear instead of the brown and white polka-dot dress Geraldine had laid out the night before.

"But, baby," Geraldine chuckled, "remember you'll have your choir robe on. So if you wear something special, nobody'll see it."

"But, Mama, *I'll* know," Doris said rather forcefully. "And didn't Daddy tell you he's taking us out for Chinese food to celebrate?"

"Yes, he did, and you are absolutely right. So go on upstairs and pick yourself out something special to wear," said Geraldine, barely able to suppress another chuckle.

Doris raced upstairs and began looking feverishly through her closets and dresser drawers. The first thing she grabbed was a pair of white tights.

A little while later Doris heard the doorbell ring, and then she heard her mother say, "Why, good mornin', Carrie." Doris hastily tucked her blouse in her skirt. As she reached for her shoes she heard her godmother say:

"Geraldine, I was halfway up the church steps before I realized I didn't have the new runner for the communion table. Then it dawned on me that I'd left it in the bag with those doilies I picked up for you the other day."

"Now where did I put that bag? . . . Just wait right here one little minute," Geraldine said as she headed up the stairs. Half a minute later, Doris was at the top of the stairs in her favorite outfit: her royal blue velveteen suit and her white blouse with the Puritan collar.

"Good morning, Sister Carrie."

"Mornin', sugar. My, my, my! Don't you look sharp today!"

"Thank you. I picked my outfit out myself because it's a special — "

"I heard, I heard! And I'm just as happy as I can be for you in your special outfit on your special day."

When Doris's black patent leather T-straps reached the bottom step, Sister Carrie moved to tuck Doris's blouse in all the way.

"Here it is, Carrie," Geraldine said as she came down the stairs.

"Mama, I'm all ready. Can I go with Sister Carrie now? Please-please."

"Did you ask her if she'd mind having some company?"

"You bet she did," said Sister Carrie, giving Doris a wink. "And I told her it was better than fine because I could use a little helper this morning."

Doris raced upstairs and then back down with her coat. As she headed through the front door behind Sister Carrie, Geraldine called out softly, "Doris, don't forget your choir robe."

"Thank you, Mama." Doris removed her robe from the coatrack, and over her shoulder tossed out, "And, Mama, don't worry. I won't get it all wrinkled."

Geraldine stood in the doorway and watched Doris and Sister Carrie go down the front steps, hand in hand. Her eyes followed them as far as the corner. Sister Carrie — head up, shoulders back — walking tall and briskly; Doris, trying her best to keep pace with her. "Good Lord," Geraldine said as she closed the front door. "That Carrie Cole sure is something else."

When Carrie Cole joined Mt. Calvary she shuddered every time someone called her "Sister Cole" because it sounded too stiff, too serious. "Just call me, 'Sister Carrie'," she said politely but firmly. And everybody did — everybody except her long-time friend Geraldine.

Sister Carrie was one of Mt. Calvary's most active members. She served as mistress of ceremonies for special events. She was president, vice president, secretary, treasurer, and sole member of the Church

Beautification Committee. She was also the church's star singer and, next to Geraldine, the only one allowed to free-lance with the choir.

On top of it all, Sister Carrie was also *the* fashion plate of Mt. Calvary.

Today she had on a bright butterscotch wool single-breasted suit with wide shoulders. Down below she sported black suede pumps with a three-inch heel and, on the toe, a black satin camellia with a cluster of round rhinestones in the center. Tiny rhinestones rode up the seams of her silk stockings. On her head was a wide-brimmed black felt fedora with a fanciful arrangement of peacock feathers and black ostrich plumes around the crown. A black net veil sprinkled with teeny-tiny rhinestones cascaded down the front and fell just below the freckles that traced along Sister Carrie's cheekbones.

Many women at Mt. Calvary took their fashion cues from Sister Carrie. And many others, of course, reproached her for the way she dressed.

"Too worldly!" some grumbled.

"Too much color!" others sniped.

"Who does she think she is?" muttered still others.

To those who criticized her to her face, Sister Carrie usually responded, "Why shouldn't I put on my best for the Lord?" or "God don't want his children dragging around in sackcloth and ashes."

Born with an extra helping of charisma, Sister Carrie had developed grace and elegance as a blues singer years before. When she left show business and settled in Harlem, she opened a beauty parlor

on Seventh Avenue and 133rd Street: Carrie's Twirl
'N' Curl. Doris loved to visit the shop. She marveled
at the way Sister Carrie kept the beauticians and
manicurists on their toes, seeing to it that her shop
was clean and in order.

And a Saturday afternoon at Sister Carrie's apartment was a trip to wonderland. Sister Carrie told
Doris story after story about her days in show business singing with Frank Long, the Carter Bunch Jazz
Sentinels, the Jimmy Knight Orchestra, and other
bands. Doris could taste the glamour. Sister Carrie's
storytelling was nothing short of a performance.
Doris sat in awe as Sister Carrie sang her favorite
tunes and put on what amounted to a fashion show
to capture for Doris the spirit of the times, the night,
the audience. Doris occasionally got in on the act
and pranced around in Sister Carrie's furs, scarves,
shawls, and jewelry.

Sister Carrie was no less dramatic when she was
teaching Doris church songs. One of Doris's favor-
ites was "There's No Place to Hide." It was a song
that filled Doris to the brim with joy. Sister Carrie
always ended the song by sweeping her arms open
wide and holding her head up, up, up.

Whether she was reminiscing about her days in
show business or practicing songs for church, Sister
Carrie always instructed Doris in the proper way to
carry herself. One of her frequent reminders was,
"Doris, you're slouching. Now stand up straight,
push your shoulders back, and pretend that there
is an invisible string attached to the top of your head
pulling you up to a higher plane."

For Doris, Sister Carrie was like a second mother

and a big sister rolled into one. Deep down inside Doris knew no one could replace her mother. There was no better sleep than when Doris dozed off onto her mother's bosom, which gave up the light scent of her honeysuckle talc. Whenever Doris caught a cold, it was her mother who chased the sick-bug away with spoonfuls of chicken and dumplings, and rubbed her down and into a warm sleep with camphor balm.

Geraldine was Doris's fortress. But Sister Carrie was the extras: a piece of chewing gum or peppermint candy on the sly in church; a banana split after service; a trip to the zoo and more popcorn and cotton candy than Geraldine would have allowed. And she always gave Doris the nicest presents. Whenever she received a present from Sister Carrie, Doris was always overjoyed, but rarely surprised. Around Doris's birthday or Christmas, Sister Carrie would take Doris "pretend shopping" on 125th Street or in one of the department stores downtown. At every store she'd ask, "If you could have anything in this store . . . ?" Doris was never fooled. Weeks later, when Sister Carrie came by with a present, she knew it was bound to be one of the "anythings" she had picked out, like the royal blue velveteen suit Doris had on this morning.

"Sister Carrie?" Doris asked as they walked up Lenox Avenue. "The first time you sang in front of a lot of people, were you nervous?"

"Of course, sugar. Second time, too. But I soon learned that nervousness can get in the way of your talent. It's human to get nervous, so the trick is handling it."

"And how do you do that?"

"Years ago, just before I went on, I used to run through a song ten times quickly in my head. Now I don't bother with all that. I just say a little prayer asking God to direct my voice. Then I take two deep breaths and I relax my shoulders. When the music starts, I just let myself ease on into it."

"You mean you let the music take control? That's what Brother Wesley is always telling us to do?"

"Exactly."

"Then what do I do — I mean, what do you do after you let the music take control?" Doris asked.

"Well, I remind myself that there's somebody out there who needs to be touched, to be healed, and that my singing is a channel for that healing."

Doris and Sister Carrie walked a few steps in silence.

"You see, sugar plum," Sister Carrie added as they reached 130th Street, "you must always remember that singing is another way of giving. It's not just showing off a talent, but it's giving people something."

"For keeps?"

"Yeah, for keeps."

Doris loved being Sister Carrie's little helper at the church. Her favorite job was arranging the altar flowers. Second to that she loved laying out the communion table, which was all set except for the chalice when Geraldine entered the sanctuary.

"Doris," said Geraldine, "I think it's about time you go and join the choir in the rehearsal room."

"Where's Daddy?"

"He went straight to his office through the side

door," Geraldine replied as she helped Doris into her robe.

"Mama, where's your robe?"

"I'm not singing today, precious. I want to sit out here and watch my baby sing. Now go on."

As Doris headed downstairs, Sister Carrie headed for Reverend Winter's office to get the chalice.

When Sister Carrie entered the office, Reverend Winter was standing behind his desk putting on his white robe.

"Good morning, Sister Carrie," Reverend Winter said cheerfully.

"Good mornin', Rev," Sister Carrie replied as she made her way across the room. As she removed the chalice from the cabinet, she heard a gasp and a sharp, quick "ooh!" When she turned around, she saw Reverend Winter easing into his chair with his hand pressed hard over the left side of his chest.

"Are you all right, Rev?"

"I'm fine, Sister Carrie. Just fine. Probably just a touch of indigestion, that's all."

"Rev, that looked like a little more than a little indigestion."

"Sister Carrie, Lord knows I appreciate your concern, but if you're looking for something to fret about, you're just going to have to look elsewhere," Reverend Winter said with a smile. "But I will ask one favor of you. Would you sing my favorite song in service this morning?"

Sister Carrie knew he meant "Faith Can Move a Mountain," and she could also tell from his face and his voice that he really needed to hear that song.

"Why, of course, Rev," she said, giving him a

good, long look. "My pleasure," she added as she moved to leave the office.

"And Sister Carrie . . ."

"Yes, Rev?"

"You're the finest godmother Doris could ever have."

"Why, thank you, Rev."

"Promise me you'll always be there for her, and help her in any way you can. You know, always look out for her."

"Why, of course, Rev," Sister Carrie said with a slight tremble in her voice.

Doris felt her stomach drop when she heard the first chords of the processional hymn. But once she began to sing, no more nervousness. Before she knew it, she was down the aisle and up on the choir stand in her very own blue and white robe. During the announcements, Doris saw her mother with that I'm-so-proud-of-my-baby smile on her face, and noticed that Sister Carrie, seated next to her, seemed to be fidgeting more than usual. From the choir stand the congregation looked different to Doris. Just last week, she thought, I was down there watching the choir and singing along with them from the pews. And now . . . Doris broke off her musings when she heard Reverend Grady say, "Now we will have a special selection from Sister Carrie. And then the next voice you will hear will be that of our pastor, Reverend Randolph A. Winter."

As Sister Carrie made her way to the front, her eyes met Reverend Winter's. He nodded slightly. She returned his nod with a nervous half-smile.

"Our beloved pastor has requested this morning that I sing his favorite song," Sister Carrie announced to the congregation. As the organist rolled down the keyboard and into the first chords of the song, Sister Carrie began to hum the melody softly and sway from side to side.

"Now you know the Lord saved me and then He raised me by faith. And I'm here this morning to tell you, church, that you cannot please the Lord without faith."

"Tell it, Sister Carrie. Tell it!" someone shouted out.

With the congregation revved up, Sister Carrie took off on the song:

> *Faith can move a mountain.*
> *Faith can open any door.*
> *Faith will help you find the answer. . . .*

As Sister Carrie stretched out on the song the congregation spurred her on with "Go 'head girl!" and "Sing it, sister, sing it!" and "Don't hold back, now!"

At one point Reverend Winter rose from his chair with a hearty "Yeeaaaah!" and an "Oh, yeeess!" The congregation backed him up with "Amen!" and the organist soloed for a while. Sister Grier whipped out her tambourine and jingle-jangled away. Then Sister Carrie picked up the song again and belted out "Faith!" and swept the whole church on its feet and into the song.

As Doris sang out boldly along with everyone else about the mysterious power of faith, she felt something she had never felt before: a closeness to all around her. And she wondered if she would ever be able to move people with her singing the way Sister Carrie had.

As Sister Carrie brought the song to a close, Reverend Winter exclaimed, "Oh, yes!" As the applause waned, he moved to the podium and said, "Let us thank the lovely Sister Carrie for that song of inspiration this morning, for truly, truly, faith is what we need. . . . Let the church say 'Amen.' "

And the church said "Amen" and "Amen" and "Amen."

The "Amens" died down and the church grew quiet except for Sister Grier's occasional "Hallelujah" and the stray rattle of her tambourine. Reverend Winter's eyes rested on Geraldine, then on Sister Carrie, and then he turned to the choir stand, and his eyes lingered on Doris.

"My text for today," said Reverend Winter as he faced the congregation, "is taken from Ephesians. Chapter four, verse one. And it reads like this: 'I therefore, the prisoner of the Lord, beseech you that ye walk worthy of the vocation wherewith ye are called.' " As his eyes roamed the pews he asked, "What does that mean? . . . As I see it, it means that inside you, inside me, inside *every* human being, there is a talent, a calling. . . . And so it becomes our duty — our one and only duty — to discover, *un*cover and *re*cover this talent, this calling."

Beads of perspiration on Reverend Winter's forehead were beginning to turn into streams. He brought out a handkerchief from underneath his robe and wiped it across his brow.

"Now I am here to remind you — and sometimes, yes, I have to remind myself — that we have all we need right here inside ourselves. Yes, inside every man, woman, and child — " Here, Reverend Winter turned and gestured toward Doris. " . . . there is a voice, a living spirit that can guide us and *will* guide us anytime we listen. We can know that we are at one with the Almighty, All-Powerful . . . God!"

As "God" left Reverend Winter's lips, he hunched over and clutched the left side of his chest. This time he was unable to make it to a chair, but collapsed onto the floor.

"Daddy!" Doris screamed. In a flash she was at her father's side. Geraldine was not far behind.

"Dor — Doris, pump . . . kin. I love you. . . . Walk worthy of — " When Reverend Winter broke off, he just stared at Doris. Doris stared back into his peaceful eyes. Then a chill swept over her entire body.

Mass confusion, mass hysteria swept through the sanctuary. Over the gasps, sobs, screams, and jagged movements, what stood out above all else was Doris's wail, "DAAADDY! DADDY! DADDY! NOOOOOOO!"

Five

By eleven o'clock that next Sunday morning, there was standing room only at Mt. Calvary Full Gospel Church. The air was heavy with body heat and sorrow.

Doris sat in the first pew on the right, between her mother and Sister Carrie, counting the flower arrangements that stretched across the width of the church and had turned the pulpit into a garden. By the time she reached 108, the first chords of "We've Come This Far by Faith" made her lose count. She thought of starting again. Instead, she just stared at the casket spray. As she did, her mind began to wander and snag on the oddest things. She noticed for the first time that the letters *F-U-N* were at the beginning of the word "funeral." When she heard the choir sing "My Faith Looks Up to Thee," she thought of how she had always looked up to her

father. She wondered if she still could. And if so,
how?

Doris's wonderings were now and then inter-
rupted by different peoples' voices and their words:
"Pillar of the community . . . Mighty man of God
. . . Friend in a time of need . . . Beloved Pastor . . .
Randolph Adolphus Winter . . ."

With her eyes still fixed on the casket, the next
voice Doris heard was her own. "Mama . . ."

"Yes, Doris?"

"Mama, I want to sing."

"Go ahead, child. . . . Sing for your father."

Doris moved stiffly to the casket and looked down
at her father. Then she faced front. Timidly, softly,
she began to sing:

> . . . When Jesus is my portion?
> My constant Friend is He:
> His eye is on the sparrow,
> And I know he watches me.

There was silence in the sanctuary. But beneath
it, the congregation was praying Doris through the
song. With each verse, Doris's voice grew steadier
and steadier; with each verse, she felt a little bit
stronger. But when she finished singing, she hardly
felt it when her mother pressed her to her bosom
and led her back to her seat. She hadn't smelled
the honeysuckle. She did not shed a tear.

The line of people that wound past the casket,
past the family section, and then out of the church

seemed endless. When people stopped to shake Geraldine's hand and pat Doris on the head, Doris never looked up. She counted shoes. Two hundred and one . . . Two hundred and two . . . Two hundred and three. . . . When Doris did look up, she saw the undertaker closing the casket.

No, Doris said to herself.

"No!" Doris shouted as she rose from her seat.

"NOOOO!" she screamed as she raced to the casket and pushed the undertaker away.

"No! No! No!" she cried. "Don't take my daddy away! Don't take my daddy away!"

Doris's wrenching sobs echoed through the sanctuary. Her father was gone forever.

As is usually the case, grief did not come all at once. It strung itself out over time. Doris stood by listlessly as waves of people overran her home. She watched every flat surface in the kitchen grow into a mound of food. She stared at the hungry, gobbling it down on the spot. She glared at the greedy, piling it into pie pans and paper plates, wrapping it up to take home. Doris hated the avalanche of people. Of food. Relatives and family friends suddenly seemed strangers. Busybodies. Vultures. Doris flinched when she heard them ask Geraldine for a little something of Reverend Winter's. Something to remember him by: a pair of cuff links, a tie clip, a photograph. Everybody wanted a piece of her daddy. And they wanted a piece of Doris, too. These strangers tweaked her nose. They planted slobbery kisses on her cheeks, her forehead. They bombarded her

with "you po' baby" this and "you po' baby" that.
They forced hugs and kisses out of Doris in return.

Doris cringed whenever someone started talking
about her father. When others joined in to boast
about how well they knew him and lie about what
he said to them when last they met, she left the
room. Doris wanted to smash Sister Grier in the face
with her tambourine every time she collared somebody to tell about the dream she had the night before
Reverend Winter died. "He was riding in a silver
chariot with diamonds and rubies. Jus' as clearly as
I see yo' face, I seen him enter the Pearly Gates."

Yes, Doris wanted to smash Sister Grier in the
face a hundred times. Until the bottom of her tambourine busted. Until the jinkles clinked to the floor.
Next to that, Doris wanted to be alone. And more
than anything else . . . Doris wanted to know why
her father was gone.

"Brother Wesley, why did my daddy have to die?"

"My dear, do not think of your father as having
died. He has only been translated into glory."

"A lot of good that does me," Doris muttered.

"And remember, my dear, you still have your
mother and the rest of us. And you always have the
Lord. And as the songwriter wrote, 'God will be'."

God may be my Heavenly Father, she thought, but
he can't ever be my daddy.

"Sister Carrie, why did my daddy have to die?"

"Sugar, we all have to go sometime. Your daddy's
time came a little bit sooner than we expected. But

he'll always be with us in spirit. And remember that your daddy would want all of us to go on and live our lives to the fullest."

"But now there'll always be something missing. How can life ever be full?"

"Mama? Mama, why did Daddy die? He was good. He served the Lord with all his heart, mind, and strength. Why couldn't he have a chance to grow old? I heard somebody say old man Kennedy across the street been drunk every day of his life and chase women every night. How come he got a chance to get old?"

"Baby, the Lord moves in mysterious ways. His ways are not our ways. The Lord giveth and the Lord taketh away."

"Mama, what kind of God takes a daddy away from his little girl?"

No one could tell Doris why her daddy died, because no one had the answer.

With this unanswered question gnawing at her insides, Doris grew angrier and angrier. Then Anger sent her for a visit with Guilt.

Maybe if I hadn't asked for all those new things for Christmas, she thought, he wouldn't have had to work so hard and maybe . . . I wonder if I'd helped more with the chores around the house, maybe he could have gotten more rest and . . . Maybe if I hadn't asked him to carry me upstairs the night before he died . . . He said I was getting heavy. . . . Maybe I strained his heart.

And then Guilt abandoned Doris and left her alone to be numb.

Three days after the funeral, Geraldine began to sort through her husband's things. Doris hated her mother all day long.

"Mama, why are you doing this? It's like you throwing Daddy away!"

"Baby, it's not like that at all. But some of his things got a whole lot more wearing in them. He'd want somebody who could use them to have them."

"You giving away his robes, too?" Doris hissed.

"No, baby, I'm not letting go of your father's robes."

The deacons came to the house to take the things being given away over to the church. Doris plopped down on the middle of the staircase and folded her arms over her chest.

"Baby, move so they can get by," was all Geraldine said.

When Deacon Branch hobbled into her father's study, Doris stormed in after him. She shot invisible darts into his neck as he ran his finger down the spines of a few of Reverend Winter's books. Doris began to seethe when he removed one from the shelf and lowered himself into Reverend Winter's armchair.

"You can't sit there!" Doris spat out, and then stomped over, snatched the book from his hand and added, "And you can't have his book!"

Deacon Branch hobbled out of the room without further ado.

The deacons descended the stairs. Doris stood at

the bottom of the stairs and scowled at them one
by one as they passed her by with pieces of her
daddy. In cardboard boxes. In shopping bags.

That night Doris pulled out her composition book
with the song her father had given her. She stared
at the words: "Follow the dream. . . . In you I see
the gift of song. . . . Just have the faith. . . . Just be
yourself as you truly could be . . . my little girl."

Doris didn't want to dream, and she couldn't care
less if she ever sang again. All Doris wanted was to
be her father's little girl. She tucked the composition
book under her pillow and cried herself to sleep.

Six

Geraldine tried not to let Doris see her cry a lot, and Doris took it as a sign of a cold heart. She felt better when she saw Geraldine cock her head to the side and stare into space as she wiped a dishrag across the kitchen counter, or drum her fingers on the arm of the couch in the parlor. Then Doris knew her mother was thinking about her daddy. But when Geraldine caught Doris staring at her during these moments, she began to rattle on about nothing as if trying to change the subject. Doris again thought her mother heartless.

Doesn't she like to think about him? Doris wondered.

Of course, Geraldine thought about her husband every other minute of the day. Yet she knew she could not afford to sit in the house staring with unseeing eyes at photographs of her beloved, remembering mementos, and wearing black. That, she knew, would not be good for her or Doris. She knew she had to go on with the business of living. As Geraldine thought about the bills coming due soon and the ones to come down the road, she knew she would have to mourn while she kept in motion, mourn while she worked.

Unbeknownst to Geraldine, the deacons and church officers gathered together and voted unanimously to offer Geraldine a salary to do the same administrative work she had been doing all these years for free. Geraldine accepted the offer for the blessing that it was, but she didn't want to spend the rest of her life "just barely makin' it." And so, as Geraldine sat at the kitchen table snapping green beans on a rainy mid-March afternoon, she decided to take in tenants again.

"So long, spare rooms," she said, cocking her head to the side. And as her mind traveled to the floor below, she sighed, "And, Rev, looks like we're never going to have that recreation room."

The next morning, Geraldine walked over to the *Amsterdam News* and placed an ad in the paper for the two rooms on the third floor. Two days later she met with a local contractor to get an estimate on converting the rooms downstairs into an apartment.

While Geraldine moved on with her plans, Doris remained stuck on pause.

When she opened the front door one day and found two ladies with silly grins on their faces and the *Amsterdam News* under their arms, she knew what they wanted. Mumbling "Just a minute," she let the door close in their faces and called out drily,

"Mama, it's for you." As she walked upstairs she heard Geraldine apologize for her daughter's behavior as she led the grinning ladies into the parlor.

In a way, Doris was relieved when Geraldine told her over dinner that Miss Lucille Anderson and her cousin Miss Lula Mae Wilkins would be moving in at the end of the week, and she thought: At least there'll be no more strange people ringing our doorbell. When Geraldine explained that both women had sleep-in jobs and would only be around on their day off, then Doris thought: Good, I won't have to see their grinning faces every day.

Doris continued to drift through her days in a cloak of sadness. At school, if she knew the right answer to a math problem or the date of an historic event, she often mumbled, "I don't know" when called upon. And she never raised her hand in class, not even in English, which had been her favorite subject. Social studies had always bored her. Now it bored her more. If she played with Toni after school, she let Toni win a lot at jacks and carelessly stepped on the lines when they played hopscotch in front of her house. When Sister Carrie stopped by on a Saturday morning with "Come on, sugar, come watch me do some hair," or a Sunday morning with, "Doris, I sure could use a little helper this morning," the few times Doris went along she remained quiet and detached. Whenever Sister Carrie took her out pretend shopping, there weren't too many "anythings" that struck her fancy. In fact, Doris was learning not to want anything in life.

The last thing in the world she wanted to do was go to church. She dreaded Mt. Calvary. People were still giving her those creepy pity-looks and being sugary nice for no reason, and asking her that dumbest of questions: "How you holdin' up?" And the worst part was seeing Reverend Grady in her father's chair in the pulpit.

Wednesday by Wednesday, Doris lost interest in the choir. And it showed.

One evening Geraldine found Doris sprawled across her bed when she should have been getting ready for choir rehearsal. "Doris, you better get a move on."

"Do I have to go?" Doris moaned.

"What kind of question is that?"

"I just don't feel like . . . I, uh, got a sore throat."

"Sore throat, my foot. You just letting yourself slump into one of those black moods of yours. And sit up and look at me when I'm talking to you." Geraldine thought she saw Doris cut her eyes at her but she wasn't sure, so she let it slide. "Come on now, get moving. Choir rehearsal will take your mind off your blues. And if your throat is really sore, you can still listen and learn something. . . . Or are your ears sore, too? . . . They must be because you don't seem to hear so good this evening. I *said* get moving!"

Doris huffed, "Yes, Mama," and reached for her shoes. As Geraldine turned from the room, she thought she heard Doris suck her teeth and say something about somebody "makes me sick." Geraldine thought that somebody was she, and headed back into the room ready to slap Doris into tomorrow. But Geraldine held her hand and tried to hold in her anger.

"Doris, you workin' my last nerve. Keep it up and more than your throat will be sore."

Doris and Geraldine went to rehearsal with a stone wall of silence between them.

At choir rehearsal, Doris didn't half speak to anyone, didn't half listen to the Minister of Music, and didn't half try to sing. When rehearsal was over, the Minister of Music took Doris aside.

"My dear, you were having a lot of problems tonight. You seemed to be having trouble concentrating."

"Sorry," sighed Doris.

"And this isn't the first time."

"I *said* I'm sorry, what more do you — "

Doris never finished the sentence, because suddenly the whole right side of her face was stinging hot, her vision blurred, and for a few seconds she didn't know where she was. After a few blinks she realized what had happened. It was that notorious mother-slap that comes out of nowhere and travels at the speed of light. Doris turned to her right and there stood Geraldine glowering down at her.

"I've had just about enough of this attitude, Doris. Now apologize to Brother Wesley."

I will not cry, Doris said to herself, I will not cry.

"That's quite all right, Sister Winter. If you don't mind, I'd just like to have a few minutes alone with Doris."

Geraldine stepped aside and fumed, both embarrassed and in agony that her child was so bound up with sorrow.

* * *

"Sister Winter," said the Minister of Music a few minutes later, as he and Doris walked over to Geraldine, "Doris and I both agree that Doris should leave the choir. Please know that there are no hard feelings."

"But, but — " Geraldine's objection began. But then something inside said, Leave it alone, Geraldine. Leave it alone.

Doris's eyes were on the pavement all the way home. She never looked up, not even when she whispered, "Mama, I'm sorry, but I just don't want to be in the choir. Singing is just not the same anymore."

"Okay, Doris, okay," Geraldine whispered back.

Spring became summer. The swelter of summertime fizzled into fall. In October, Doris knew a few sunny days, but then came the holidays. And the holidays were unbearable.

When Doris, Geraldine, and Sister Carrie sat down at the dining room table for a sumptuous Thanksgiving feast, the only thing Doris hungered for was the sight of her father saying grace, carving the turkey, and serving himself a big piece of his favorite dessert, pumpkin pie. When Christmas came, Doris couldn't wait for it to go: she was at a loss for any good tidings and she could feel no great joy. In January, Geraldine gave Doris a party for her twelfth birthday. Doris ate too much strawberry shortcake along with the other children and played party games. She shined a little, but not for long.

By the end of the month, the apartment down-

stairs had been completed and Geraldine rented it
to a Miss Plato, a nurse at Harlem Hospital. She
was a trim and cheerful young woman who radiated
cleanliness. Doris wanted to like her, but she
wouldn't allow herself to. Like the other tenants,
Miss Plato was a constant reminder of just how
much everything had changed.

And then, on April 1, Doris had a strange dream.

She was sitting in the back of Mt. Calvary. The
church was pitch-black and empty. An invisible
choir was singing "We've Come This Far by Faith."
The singing grew louder and louder. Doris pressed
her hands over her ears and buried her head in her
lap. When she did this, she heard muffled screams:
"Nooooo! Don't take my daddy away!" When she
removed her hands from her ears, there was a moment of silence. Then again she heard faintly "We've
Come This Far by Faith." Louder and louder. Stop.
A hazy light swept across the pulpit. Doris saw her
father sitting in the armchair from his study. He was
wearing his white robe. Doris charged up the center
aisle. Midway up, she started moving in slow motion. Out of nowhere a howling wind began to blow.
The wind had tiny slivers of ice that looked like the
rhinestones on the seams of Sister Carrie's stockings. Doris bowed her head. She pressed on through
the wind, through the rhinestones. Finally the wind
stopped howling. Then it stopped blowing. Doris
found herself in the pulpit clutching her father's
robe. Reverend Winter was gone. Doris buried her
head in her father's robe, sobbing, clutching it
tighter and tighter. Then she saw the Minister of

Music marching up the aisle toward her, singing "God Will Be."

Over his singing, she heard words that seemed familiar, yet new. "My firstborn child . . . in you I see the gift of song. . . ." Then Doris heard someone whisper, "Be not afraid. . . . The dream's the start. . . . No need to moan. . . . No need to suffer. Let go. Let go. . . . Trust in God."

The Minister of Music was in the pulpit standing before Doris with open arms. "Give me the robe, Doris. Give me the robe."

Doris took a few steps back and froze, unable to move. She reached out to the Minister of Music and let him take the robe from her hands.

Doris awoke in a sweat and sat bolt upright. Her first impulse was to run to her mother's room. But then, she grew calm. She felt steady. She felt clean. Doris lay back down and into a peaceful sleep.

One evening a few days later, when Doris was up in her room yawning over her social studies homework, Sister Carrie stopped by.

"Hey, Carrie. How you doing?" Geraldine asked.

"Fair to middlin'," sighed Sister Carrie as she made her way through the front door.

"Sounds like you need to come on in here to the kitchen for a piece of pie and a cup of coffee."

"Just the coffee, thank you. Last week I went to put on my lime green suit and, honey, I couldn't but halfway zip up the skirt." As sister Carrie dropped into a chair, she added, "Looks like the Lord's calling me to go on a fast."

"Hey, Sister Carrie," Doris said, entering the kitchen.

"Hello, sugar plum. Whatcha know good?" said Sister Carrie as she flung an arm around Doris's waist.

"Nothing much."

"Well, you better go find yourself some something."

With a cup of coffee in front of her, Sister Carrie turned to Geraldine. "Girl, today was a day and a half. When I went in this morning to open up the shop, what do I discover but that the hot water heater is busted. The super had it working again by noon, but by then you don't know how many pots of water I had boiled. On top of this, Sherry called in sick, so there I was juggling her appointments and mine." Between one sip of coffee and the next, Sister Carrie shifted in her chair and rolled her eyes up to the ceiling. Geraldine caught the signal and turned to Doris, "Did you finish your homework?"

"Almost."

"Almost isn't finished. Go on back upstairs and get finished."

"But I need a break. Social studies is so boring."

"Can't be as boring as being on punishment."

Doris darted from the kitchen and up the stairs.

"Geraldine, guess you know by now I didn't come over here to complain about my day. You see, early this morning I got this idea. I was thinking — "

When she broke off, she tiptoed over to the kitchen door and kicked loose the door stopper. As the door swung closed, she and Geraldine began to whisper.

* * *

At breakfast the next day, Geraldine reminded Doris that the Jubilee Concert was that coming Saturday afternoon.

"I know you didn't want to enter this year, but you don't have anything against going, do you?"

"No, I don't mind going."

Throughout the year — in the Christmas and Easter pageants, and on other occasions — the young people at Mt. Calvary had many opportunities to display their talents. But the Jubilee Concert was something extra-special. The event was open to young people ages twelve through sixteen. First prize was a twenty-five dollar savings bond; second prize, a fifteen-dollar savings bond. There was a grab bag of toys, games, books, and other goodies for the rest of the participants. Afterward, everyone was treated to ice cream and cake downstairs in the cafeteria.

The morning of the concert, Doris laid out her burgundy and white plaid dress.

"Baby, why don't you wear something else this afternoon?" prodded Geraldine as she proceeded to flip through Doris's closet. "What about this little outfit Carrie bought you?" she said, holding out a candy pink satin dress with puffed sleeves and a white eyelet pinafore.

A little left-out feeling tugged at Doris's heart as she listened to Ricky Jones and Joe Parks harmonizing on "Swing Low, Sweet Chariot," and Julie Walker stirring up the crowd with her violin solo of

"Joshua Fit the Battle of Jericho." She really felt a pang of regret that she had not entered as Linda Miles moved the crowd into glory with "Mary, Don't You Weep."

Stevie Lee's drum solo brought the concert to a close. Steady applause accompanied him as he took his seat among the other participants. Then Sister Carrie, as mistress of ceremonies, took center stage once again in a turquoise taffeta dress that was fitted to the waist and then flared out from there on down to her open-toed, silver sling-back shoes. Silver satin gloves rose to her elbows. Large crystal teardrops framed in brushed silver dangled from her ears.

"Let us give all our young people a hearty round of applause for their very fine and moving performances here tonight in our Sixth Annual Young People's Jubilee Concert!" said Sister Carrie as she signaled the participants to stand and take a bow. "And," she continued as the applause died down, "after seeing what these very gifted young people have done today, I would like to make a little contribution to this program on behalf of my once and forever young self."

When Doris heard the melody of the song, her eyes sparkled, and as Sister Carrie began to sing, Doris began to beam.

> *He'll be your strength.*
> *He'll be your guide.*
> *There's no reason to falter.*
> *There's no place to hide. . . .*

Sister Carrie motioned for Doris to join her. Doris looked to her right, then back up at Sister Carrie, then to Geraldine on her left.

"Mama!" she gasped. "Is Sister Carrie calling for me?"

"Sure looks that way to me."

"But, Mama — "

"But Mama nothing. Go on up there and see what your godmother wants."

Sister Carrie signaled the piano player to play softly. Over the music she said, "I'd just like to continue this song with a little help from my friend, Doris."

The audience encouraged Doris out of her seat with handclaps and the rustle of "Oh, isn't that sweet." As Doris made her way forward, Sister Carrie signaled the piano player to bring the music back up. With Doris by her side, Sister Carrie sang another verse. Then she twisted the microphone from its stand and handed it to Doris. Doris sang one verse with a touch of the jitters in her voice. Doris handed the microphone back, but Sister Carrie, with her hands on her hips and a shake of her head, refused it.

"I *know* you can do better than that, Doris? Can't she, y'all?"

"Sure she can. . . . Show her what you made of. . . . Don't hold back now," the audience responded over their applause.

Doris accepted the challenge. She sang with spunk and pizzazz. Then she extended the microphone to Sister Carrie. This time, with a sidelong glance that said, "So there!"

Sister Carrie soared into another verse and began to strut. As she sang, she high-stepped across the floor. She bent her knees slightly for the low notes. With a little shimmy, she grew tall and straight again for the high notes. A shake of her head sent her crystal earrings into a tizzy.

By the time Sister Carrie was halfway through another verse, the very last trace of the cloud that had hung over Doris for fifteen long months vanished. But when Sister Carrie prodded Doris to match her in song *and* movements, Doris felt that hiding feeling creep back up on her: Oh, Lord, she thought, I can't do all that stuff! Doris looked out frantically at her mother with eyes that said, "Help!" Geraldine's eyes answered her with a look that said, "She ain't got a thing on you, baby girl!"

Doris moved over to Sister Carrie and rose to the occasion. She matched her note for note, strut for strut, shimmy for shimmy. She soloed for a while and found notes, twists, and turns that surprised even herself. Sister Carrie joined Doris for the last verse of the song and with perfect breathing, harmony, pitch, and control, they ended the song with a resounding:

THERE'S NO PLACE TO HIDE!

Just like Sister Carrie, Doris swept her arms out wide and held her head up, up, up.

During the applause, Doris felt all tingly — from the top of her head to the soles of her feet. Doris got the message in the music. A new mood was upon her.

"Mama?" Doris chirped as she and Geraldine entered the front door later that evening. "Can we have something fun for dinner like . . . like, bacon, lettuce, and tomato sandwiches?"

"With a thin slice or two of red onion?" Geraldine added with a conspiratorial wink.

"No onions for me, but I'll take a piece of cheese." Doris winked back.

"Sounds good to me, but after all that ice cream and cake you had, I'm surprised you have room for anything else."

"I'm still hungry all right. I'm just not big-hungry, is all."

Doris washed the lettuce and laid out the bread and cheese. When Geraldine finished frying the bacon, she moved on to slice the tomatoes, all the while humming "Mary, Don't You Weep."

"Baby girl, baby girl!" she exclaimed, breaking off from her hum. "You sure showed out today!"

"Yeah, I did, didn't I? Oh, but I forgot!"

Doris raced upstairs and returned in a flash with her hands behind her back.

"Even though I wasn't really in the concert, Sister Bates let me get a prize out of the grab bag." Doris brought one arm forward and handed Geraldine a large barrette with three red roses. "Here, Mama, I want you to have it."

"Why bless your heart, baby. Bless your heart. . . . Lord knows it sure is nice to have you back to your old self. Did my heart more good than you'll ever know to hear you sing like that."

During a pause, Geraldine put her knife to the red onion.

"Doris, I may not know much, but there is one thing I know. God did not put us on this earth to be miserable. As day follows night, hurts, disappointments, and setbacks will come your way. Now we sure can't choose our misfortunes, but we *can* choose whether or not we're going to be miserable. And if you choose to be miserable, you can get so lost in your blues, you just might lose yourself. You'll forget about living and you'll forget about your blessings, not to mention your God-given talents, baby girl."

As Geraldine assembled the sandwiches, Doris set the table.

"And you know," Geraldine continued as she and Doris sat down to the table, "when God gives us a talent, the only way we can really say 'thank you' is by putting that talent to good use."

That week, Doris rejoined the choir. When she took her place in the soprano section, the other choir members gave her a welcome-back hand-clap — everyone except Brother Cooper, who humphed under his breath, "Had a been anybody else, they would of had to beg for weeks. . . . Just because she's Geraldine Winter's daughter. . . ."

During rehearsal it was clear that Doris's voice had not gotten out of shape at all. But her memory had. She blanked out on an entire verse of one song. On another song, she came in a little behind the beat. When Doris faltered, the Minister of Music came down hard on her. Too hard, in Doris's opinion. After all, she thought, this *is* my first day back.

Rehearsal ended a little earlier than usual. As Doris and Geraldine were preparing to leave, the Minister of Music called out, "Oh, Sister Winter, I'd like to have a few words with Doris, if you don't mind. I won't keep her long and I will, of course, bring her home."

Once everyone had gone, the Minister of Music sat Doris down at the plank-top table.

"Doris, when I heard that you wanted to come back to the choir, I rejoiced." The thought of him rejoicing made Doris smile.

"But . . ." he continued in a tone that wiped the smile off Doris's face, "I knew you would have a lot of work to do if you were to remain in the choir."

"But, Brother Wesley, I only really messed up bad on one song — "

"Yes, but you were mediocre on the others. Mediocrity may have its place some place, but not in my choir."

"But Brother Wesley," Doris stammered, almost bursting into tears, "I was — I was in mourning."

"Yes, I know. I grieved along with you. But that does not alter the fact that you have a lot of work cut out for you if you are going to catch up and prove yourself worthy of being in this choir."

This is starting to sound like school! Doris thought.

"To start with," the Minister of Music continued, removing a book and a piece of paper from his attaché case, "here is a list of the songs I have added to the choir's repertoire while you were, as you say, in mourning. You will find them all in this book. I will expect you to know the first three songs backward and forward by next week. The others, I will expect you to have down pat by the end of the month."

Doris looked down the list of sixteen songs and thought, Phew! At least there are a few I already know.

"I want you to come to rehearsal an hour early next week. That means be here at precisely six o'clock. I will go over the songs with you then."

The Minister of Music left the rehearsal room feeling accomplished; Doris feeling doomed. They walked up the basement steps in silence, the Minister of Music out in front, Doris lagging several steps behind. As he held the church door open for Doris, the Minister of Music casually said, "My dear, I assume you realize that you are on probation."

"Probation? That's like I'm a criminal or something."

"Not at all. But you do have to earn your privileges. My choir is not a revolving door. There is no going in and out at will. I must admit, I have a soft spot for you and so I bent the rules a little."

Imagine if he didn't like me! Doris thought.

"Normally I would have required a letter petitioning for reinstatement. You would have had to learn all the songs before I even considered your case. But, my dear, I decided to take a chance on you. I couldn't bear the thought of your talent going to waste any longer."

Has he been talking to my mother? Doris wondered.

After a few minutes of silence the Minister of Music said, "Doris, welcome back to the adult choir. You know, you're going to have to work hard, but I am here to serve you. I'll be your friend. I'll be your guide."

Doris and the Minister of Music walked the rest of the way in silence. When they reached the house, Doris gave him a quick hug, a cheerful "Good night," and took the steps two at a time. When she reached the top step, she spun around and added, "Thank you, Brother Wesley, thank you very much. And especially for bending the rules and letting me back in the choir so soon."

"You are most welcome, my dear. But remember, I shall not spare the rod. I will work your tail off. Understood?"

"Understood," Doris said in a chipper voice. With that, she gave the doorbell three quick jabs.

Seven

With each passing week, Doris felt better and better; she grew stronger and stronger. The difference showed everywhere she went. At school, her teachers were soon commenting on the brightness in her eyes. They began to call on her more and more in class, and Doris was now speaking up in a loud, clear voice. With Toni, she was winning again at jacks. She was once again Sister Carrie's very willing little helper at church, and when they went shopping a lot of "anythings" called out to Doris.

On her thirteenth birthday, Sister Carrie surprised her for the first time. The package she handed Doris was too small to be the yellow hat she had seen in Blumstein's and too light to be the patent leather handbag she had seen in Macy's. When she unwrapped the present, she found an ivory leather book with a border of golden curlicues. There was a little lock fitted with a tiny key. When Doris opened the book, she found that on the inside cover Sister Carrie had written:

> *To: Doris*
> *HAPPY BIRTHDAY!!!*
> *ALL MY LOVE!!!!*

Sister Carrie's signature swirled beneath these words with a flourish. On the cover page Doris read:

THIS DIARY BELONGS TO:

"Well, aren't you going to fill in your name?" Sister Carrie said with a mock scowl. She pulled out a small gold-plated pen from her handbag and added, "This goes along with it."

Trying her best to imitate Sister Carrie's fancy handwriting, Doris proudly penned her name on the line.

"Doris, you may find that from time to time you have feelings that — well, that you don't want to talk about," Sister Carrie said. "Now I'm not telling you to keep any secrets from your mama. I'm just saying that this diary is a place you can go when you need to work things out in your mind. It's also an easy way to keep a record of your life. Just think of a diary as like a silent best friend, and a very portable friend at that."

That night Doris made her first entry in her diary.

January 6, 1948

Dear Diary,

*Today is my birthday and you're a present from
Sister Carrie. She gave me a fancy pen, too.
Mama cooked me a special dinner. She made
a meat loaf in the shape of a bunny rabbit and
green beans and mashed potatoes and my favorite dessert in the world, strawberry shortcake. She also bought me some underwear and
socks. The Minister of Music gave me a book
called "Southland Spirituals." I don't have anything else to say right now. Good night.*

*P.S. What I wrote sounds kind of dumb. But I
don't know what to write. It feels funny, like
trying to have a conversation with a total
stranger. No offense, but you really don't feel
like a best friend. Not yet, anyway. Good night.
And I mean it this time.*

Doris wrote in her diary every day. Sometimes she
wrote a lot. Sometimes she couldn't think of much
to say; but even then, she always managed to write
something, and she and her diary were getting
friendlier by the day.

March 7, 1948

Dear Diary,

*Today Rev. Grady preached about Daniel in
the Lion's Den. I remember when Daddy*

preached about that. It was better when Daddy did it. Rev. Grady's sermon was okay but it wasn't like my daddy's.

April 14, 1948

Dear Diary,

Next week the choir is going to sing at Concord Baptist Church in Brooklyn. Brother Wesley said we are going to tear the house up. We are going to sing "Love Divine" and "At the Cross."

May 26, 1948

Dear Diary,

Guess what! Next week I am going to lead in the choir. At choir rehearsal Brother Wesley said he thought it was time I stretched out. Now I can tell Toni that I am broadening my horizons, too. Brother Wesley asked me what song I wanted to sing. I told him to pick. He picked "This Little Light of Mine." I invited Toni. She said she's going to come.

That Sunday, when her time came to sing, Doris felt a little flutter in her stomach, but when the music began she took a slow, deep breath and eased on into it.

> *This little light of mine,*
> *I'm going to let it shine. . . .*

Verse by verse, Doris became more relaxed and allowed the music to take total control. On the third verse, Doris stepped down from the choir stand, and as she sang she walked across the front of the church, and up and down the aisles, improvising over the choir as the spirit moved her to do. Soon she had the congregation on its feet.

> *Out in the dark,*
> *I'm going to let it shine,*
> *Oh, out in the dark,*
> *I'm going to let it shine,*
> *Hallelujah, out in the dark,*
> *I'm going to let it shine,*
> *Let it shine, let it shine, let it shine.*

Doris looked Toni's way and saw she was on her feet like everyone else, bouncing from side to side, clapping a little off time but with great gusto nonetheless.

When Doris started to bring the song to a close, the congregation refused to let her go. The womenfolk waved handkerchiefs in the air and called out, "Sing, Doris, sing!" The menfolk boomed out, "Don't stop now, girl!" Sister Grier whipped out her tambourine and yelled, "One more time!"

Doris sang the song one more time. And then one more time. As she did, her eyes and her whole self sure did shine, shine, shine.

Doris Winter was thirteen years old. That night she went to her diary. The words came straight from her heart.

June 6, 1948

Dear Diary,

I know what I want to do. I know what I want to be. I love singing. I love the audience, the clapping, the jumping, and shouting. And I know Daddy would love it, too. Oh, God, I WANT TO SING! And I don't ever, ever want to stop!

Part Two

"Travelin' Shoes"

Eight

Dear Diary,

This is my first day in West Point, Virginia. Mama sent me here to visit Aunt Francine and Uncle Riley. The train ride was fun and sometimes a little scary at night. I started missing Mama as soon as the train left New York and I can't wait until she comes down in August to join me. But Mama was right about how much of a good time I'm going to have down here because Aunt Francine and Uncle Riley sure do have a lot of land and all my cousins seem real nice. I'm going to meet more of my relatives at the big dinner they're having tonight to welcome me to West Point.

June 27, 1948

Dear Diary,

*I just love it down here. It smells so good, and
I kind of like the way people talk, the way their
words flow and curl. I can't always understand
what everybody's saying but I get most of it.
Cousin Larry said before I leave he's going to
take me to see a really big farm with a whole
lot of animals. I hope his friend Michael comes
with us. He's fifteen and lives down the road.
I met him today when he came to see Larry.
Michael Emmanuel Merriweather is his full
name. That's a name you don't mind saying a
lot, and he's sure to be blessed because Michael is one of the Archangels and Emmanuel
means, God is with us. Ain't nobody in the Bible
named Merriweather but it's a happy sounding
name at least. And Michael has the nicest
hands. He's got a scar on his right hand, but
it's a pretty one. It looks a little like a quarter
moon. And boy can he play the piano. He never
even studied neither, just plays by ear. After
dinner Aunt Francine asked him to play. She
said to me, "Doris, you ain't heard nothing until
you heard what Michael can do to a piano."
She was right. When he plays it doesn't even
look like he's trying.*

June 28, 1948

Dear Diary,

Michael came by this evening. I asked him if he was going to play for us again. He said only if I sang, because Aunt Francine told him I was the best singer in the family. I did a solo and then the whole family sang together. Everybody said they never heard nobody sing like me. Michael said I had a beautiful voice. I told him I could play the piano a little bit. Then I asked him if he could teach me some of what he knows. He said he'd start tomorrow afternoon if it was okay with Aunt Francine.

Aunt Francine said it was. And as the summer moved along, Michael proved to be an excellent teacher; and Doris, a very willing pupil.

July 30, 1948

Dear Diary,

My piano playing is getting better and better. I think Michael might be a musical genius. And he's so cute. They asked me to sing in church down here. Only if Michael plays for me, I said. Mama will be here next week. I miss her a lot but not every day.

August 13, 1948

Dear Diary,

Tomorrow me and Mama are going home. Mama was sure glad to see all her family. The

*second day she was here she started talking
more and more like them. I'm going to miss
everybody. But I think I'll miss the piano playing the most. I'm going to ask Mama if I can
start taking piano lessons from Brother Wesley
when I get back home.*

Doris came home to a house full of surprises.
Over the summer Geraldine had been very busy.

"Mama, did we get rich or something?!" Doris
exclaimed when she first laid eyes on the parlor.

With the exception of the piano and the floor
lamps, everything was new: the two-tier mahogany
coffee table and end tables; the two armchairs with
honey gold seat bottoms and scrolled arms; the
wing chair near the fireplace and the couch facing
it across the room, both of which were upholstered
in a moss green brocade. The piano was now in
front of the window that overlooked the street, and
the window had full-length honey gold draperies
with sheer white inner curtains and gold tasseled
tiebacks.

"No, baby. We're still a long way from rich, but
we're close up on a lot of blessings. The lady Miss
Lucille works for got all feverish about redoing her
house. When she asked Miss Lucille if she knew
somebody who could use this furniture, Miss Lucille
thought of us first. The drapes, I made."

Throughout the house Doris was surprised by a
lot of new things and a lot of old things Geraldine
had cleaned and fixed up like new. But the biggest
surprise of all was to come when she crossed the
threshold of her bedroom.

"Oh, Mama, I love it, I love it!" she shrieked at the sight of her white ash bedroom set with a matching desk. Jumpsy, who was in semi-retirement these days, was propped up against the headboard of her new brass bed. From the bedspread to the curtains to the crocheted doilies, the room's accenting color was powder blue.

"Mama . . ." said Doris, all choked up. "Oh, thank you, thank you."

"I'll just take one of those thank-you's. The other one belongs to your godmother."

"Can I call her up right now and thank her?"

"You can do it in person in a few hours. She'll be over for dinner."

Sister Carrie was barely through the front door before Doris was all over her with hugs, kisses, and thank-you-thank-you's. Over dinner Doris told her all about her trip down South. After dinner Doris showed Geraldine and Sister Carrie everything she had learned on the piano, and Geraldine couldn't help but say yes to piano lessons. And as if she hadn't already done enough for Doris, before Sister Carrie left, she made a date with Doris to go shopping for school clothes.

September 6, 1948

Dear Diary,

The first day of school wasn't bad. I think I'm going to like all my teachers, except for maybe my math teacher. He gave us homework. Can you believe it? I miss Toni. Her parents sent her to a school way downtown. So now I won't

get to see her every day, but Mama said I can
sleep over at Toni's house sometimes on Friday
nights.

When Doris went to spend the night at Toni's
house, Geraldine usually sent her with a pie, a cake,
or a batch of cookies. It became so habitual that
whenever Toni's little brother, John Henry, answered the door, his usual greeting was: "Hi, Doris,
whadya bring me?"

The more Doris went to Toni's house, the more
she fell in love with it. It was a limestone corner
house that narrowed after the third floor and was
capped with a mansard roof that reminded Doris of
an upside-down loaf pan. Although it was a very
spacious house with ten large rooms (and four of
them humongous), it had the feel of a cozy little
cottage. For Doris, being in the Barnett home was
like being in another world, a world where there
was so much to explore. Because Mrs. Barnett had
an extreme distaste for blank walls, throughout the
house wherever there wasn't a mirror, a bookcase,
or a tall piece of furniture, there was something on
the wall: photographs, paintings, and all kinds of
artwork. Above doorways and on crossbeams hung
all sorts of things like gourds, wooden ladles, straw
baskets, and African masks.

Doris's favorite place in the house was Mrs. Barnett's sewing room, the huge lone room on the
fourth floor. It was here that Mrs. Barnett made
dresses for her customers, many of whom were in

show business. To Doris, the room seemed like a store.

Stacked on tables and standing up in tall wicker baskets were bolts and bolts of fabric in almost every bright, pastel, and deep dark color of the rainbow: from calicos and corduroys to paisleys and plaids to velvets and voiles. Most of the wall space was taken up by floor-to-ceiling mirrors, pegboards hung with all sorts of tools and gadgets of the sewing trade, and shelving stocked with dozens of small boxes of buckles, buttons, beads, rhinestones, and sequins in assorted colors, shapes, and sizes.

Because Mrs. Barnett tended to work on several outfits at a time, Doris rarely saw any of the dress forms completely naked. At any given time, she might find the makings of a simple shirtwaist on one; on another, a suit Geraldine might wear on a Sunday; and on a third, a dress like those Sister Carrie had on in the photographs and newspaper clippings in her scrapbook. Whenever Doris visited the Barnetts, she always made a trip to the fourth floor.

One early Saturday morning, as soon as Doris entered the room she let loose an "oooh!" and darted over to a dress form wearing a cobalt blue taffeta evening gown with a plunging neckline. Here and there the dress had splashes of iridescent blue-green sequins. The shoulders, neckline, and cuffs were trimmed with ostrich feathers. A band of braided sequinned strips with a large asymmetrical blue-green brooch was sewn around the hipline.

"I think that's for someone going to a big party at

the Waldorf-Astoria," Toni volunteered with a yawn.

Doris gently lifted the skirt of the dress and held it up against herself. She looked into the mirror and imagined herself in the dress. She looked down and pointed her right foot and imagined her sneakers were silver sling-back slippers.

"Oops!" Doris said to herself when she looked back into the mirror and saw Mrs. Barnett standing in the doorway. Instantly, Doris let go of the dress and spun around with "oops!" still written all over her face.

"I'm sorry, Mrs. Barnett, but I don't think I hurt it, and my hands are clean."

"That's all right, Doris," Mrs. Barnett said as she made her way to her sewing machine. "You know, Doris, that's a good color for you. In fact, if you were older, you'd look smashing in that dress. Perhaps one day I'll make you one just like it. Would you like that?"

"Yeah, but, where would I be able to wear it to? I don't think even my godmother would wear a dress like this to church."

"Oh, Doris, when you grow up, you never know what kinds of fabulous places you'll be going to. One day you might be sailing down the Nile on the yacht of an African prince. The next day . . . sipping tea on the balcony of a palace in Monaco or Madrid."

"That'll mean you'll have to make me *two* dresses, Mrs. Barnett."

"I'll make you dozens of dresses, my little nightingale," said Mrs. Barnett as she sat down at her sewing machine. "Now, if you and Toni would be so kind as to give me some time alone, I'd be most grateful."

Doris and Toni were almost out of the room when Mrs. Barnett called them back over, and had them close their eyes and hold out their arms. She reached into a rattan trunk overflowing with assorted pieces of fabric and scraps of lace, braid, and other trimmings. Soon the girls felt their arms grow heavy. When Doris opened her eyes, she found on the top of her pile a large piece of cobalt blue taffeta and several strands of sequinned strips.

"So, now, why don't you two go into the family room and be creative," said Mrs. Barnett.

As Doris and Toni thudded down the stairs, Mrs. Barnett heard:

"I'm going to make a toga or a kimono."

"I'm going to make an evening dress, with a flowing cape and matching turban and — you think your mother might have some feathers she doesn't need?"

Second to Mrs. Barnett's sewing room, Doris loved the parlor, in part because it was the most elegant one she had ever seen, but mostly because in one corner of the room, there was a harp, a viola, a bassoon, and best of all, a baby grand piano. On the walls that formed the corner hung a balalaika, a banjo, a mandolin, a finger piano, castanets, maracas, a bottomless tambourine, and several small brass gongs.

After dinner Doris and the Barnetts often gathered in the music corner. The Barnetts taught Doris tunes from Broadway shows and other musicals. Doris taught them her favorite songs from church. Mrs.

Barnett played the piano with gusto, but badly; so everyone took up an instrument to help the music along. Doris usually reached for the tambourine; Toni, the maracas; John Henry, a gong; and Mr. Barnett plucked softly on the balalaika. In tune, off time, or right on the mark, the Barnett parlor was a sweep of laughter and delight. And Mrs. Barnett wasn't at all opposed to letting Doris teach her a thing or two on the piano.

One of the highlights of sleeping at Toni's house was sneaking out onto the second-floor landing when they were supposed to be asleep and listening in on the Barnett's company down below. When Mrs. Barnett's show business friends were over, the parlor exploded with hearty singing and laughter. And when Mr. Barnett's colleagues from City College were there, Doris and Toni overheard long serious conversations about art, religion, politics, and world events. During these times, if there was any laughter it usually had a bitter ring. Doris didn't understand everything she overheard, but she was beginning to see that the world was a far bigger place than she'd imagined.

One early Friday evening when Toni opened the front door, Doris heard hubbub coming from the parlor.

"Bon jour, mon ami! Or should I say *Bon soir?* . . . Take your stuff up to my room, then meet me in the parlor," Toni said.

"With your parents' company?"

"Of course. It's my house, too. Besides, see that buffet table across the room?"

"Yeah."

"That's dinner."

A few minutes later Toni was filling Doris in on the who, what, and where of the thirty-odd people in the room. It was a mixed crowd: skin tones ranged from blue-black to pearly white; professions ranged from artists and academicians to tradesmen and tycoons. Since the dress code for any Barnett party was not just "come as you are" but "come as whoever you wish to be," some men were dressed all the way up in tuxedos and cummerbunds, and others were dressed all the way down in turtlenecks and slacks. A few of the women had on evening dresses; a few, everyday skirts and blouses. One woman had on a pair of khaki walking shorts and an army-green battle jacket.

Toni got as far as three of the guests when she broke off with, "Excuse me, I have a question for Professor Foster."

Doris moseyed over to the buffet.

"Hello, there," said a man standing to her left.

"Good evening, sir," replied Doris, a bit entranced by his wide, easy smile and deep dark chocolate skin. The sound of his voice made her think of black velvet. Doris turned from the man when she felt a tug on her right sleeve.

"Don't eat the mushrooms," John Henry whispered. "Mommy put oysters under the stuff on top."

Doris didn't heed John Henry's warning. She tasted everything on the table. Just as she bit into a shrimp puff, from the music corner Mrs. Barnett called out:

"May I have everyone's attention for a moment,

please? . . . I trust you have all sufficiently mingled and I hope that by the end of the evening you'll have made some new friends. Most of you know my daughter, Toni — "

"And I'm her son!" John Henry shouted out from under the buffet table.

"Yes. And that's John Henry. But the reason I asked for your attention is because I'd like to introduce you to someone else, someone very special. Doris, would you come over here, please?"

Doris made her way to the music corner, chewing and swallowing quickly.

"Everyone . . . This is Doris Winter. Doris, this is everyone." Looking out at her guests, Mrs. Barnett continued, "Doris is a friend of Toni's, but we consider her family. And you should also know that she is a very accomplished singer."

A few of the guests put their hands together for a nice, polite, uptight handclap. The more down-to-earth among the crowd called out, "Hey, give us a sample. . . . How about it! . . . Yeah, come on."

"My sentiments exactly," said Mrs. Barnett, giving Doris a squeeze. "Doris, would you mind providing our guests with a little musical refreshment?"

"Well, um — okay! . . . What should I do?"

"I know!" Toni piped up. "How about 'Amazing Grace'? You're always talking about how much you like that song, and it's one Mommy knows — "

"Oh, no. That wouldn't be fair to Doris," said Mrs. Barnett. Looking out into the crowd she added, "Nat, would you be so kind as to accompany Doris?"

"My pleasure," said the man with the black velvet voice. A round of applause followed him as he made his way over to the piano. When the applause petered out, he played the opening melody, and Doris began to sing. As she did, she became amazing grace itself. When she finished singing, the parlor erupted with rapid, passionate applause.

"Do you know 'Rock of Ages'?" someone shouted out.

"Sure do!" Doris shot back.

As the man with the black velvet voice began to play, Doris leaned over to him and whispered, "Could you play it a little faster, sir? You know, pick up the tempo a bit." The man picked up the tempo with a chuckle and a wide, easy smile.

"That's it. You got it now, sir," said Doris reassuringly.

Doris began to sway from side to side with a little bounce in her step as she shifted from foot to foot. She sang the song through once, then invited everyone else to help her sing it one more time. Anyone who didn't know the song learned it quick enough because Doris sang the song using the age-old African tradition of call and response. Doris led with one line; the whole crowd echoed her.

"What's her name, again?" one woman asked her date.

"Laura Skinner," her date replied.

"Excuse me," said the woman in the khaki walking shorts. "But it's Doris Winter."

"Oh, Doris Winter," the man said. "Doris Winter. I'm going to remember that name."

That night, long after Toni had talked herself to sleep, Doris lay wide awake, still bubbling with the energy and the memory of her performance in the

Barnett parlor. It dawned on her that it was the first time she'd sung before a group of people who were for the most part total strangers. I certainly am broadening my horizons! she thought. And as she fell asleep, she let her imagination travel and began to see herself singing for the whole wide world.

When Sister Carrie picked Doris up on her way to the shop the next Saturday, Doris told her all about her evening at the Barnetts.

"You're getting to be a real little entertainer, sugar plum."

"And I wasn't one bit nervous, either."

Amid the laughter and whispers of beauty parlor talk, the click-clack of curling irons, and the smell of Bergamont and fried hair, Doris kept busy all morning long: sweeping up around the beauticians, removing the endpapers from the rollers, putting the hairpins, bobby pins, and wave clips in their proper compartments. When Doris went on a break, she took her lunch over to the love seat in the waiting area up front, and between bites flipped through the magazines lying on the table. When she came upon a hairstyle she fancied, she tried to see her face underneath it. Her imagination had to work overtime when it came to *Life*, *Look*, and some of the other magazines, because here the hairstyles were on top of white faces, and the hair itself was often blonde. She had an easier time of it when she roamed through the pages of *Ebony* because then all she had to do was imagine herself older.

Had Sister Carrie called it a day in the early afternoon, they might have dropped Doris's overnight bag off at Sister Carrie's apartment, changed their clothes, and headed back out to a gospel concert or a park. But today, by the time they left the shop, Sister Carrie was too tired to do anything more than take Doris out to dinner at Thomford's on 125th Street. When they had finished dinner they were both yawning and ready for bed, and very glad that Sister Carrie only lived a short five blocks away.

Sister Carrie had a two-bedroom apartment overlooking St. Nicholas Park, but what had sold her on the apartment was that it had lots of closets, which were the only places in her apartment she allowed any crowding. All her years on the road and changes of address had gotten her into the habit of living light. Except for a mirror or two, the walls were off-white and empty. In the entire apartment, there were no decorative little tables or wall shelving, and so no knickknacks to gather dust. Every room was sparsely furnished. The furniture in the living room consisted of an emerald green crushed velvet couch that sloped up to one side like a harp, a matching love seat nearby, and an oblong satinwood coffee table for the couch and love seat to share.

When Doris and Sister Carrie entered the apartment that night, they were improvising on a little tune Doris had hummed up, trying to outdo each other in coming up with the most clever lyrics. After they had both bathed, while Sister Carrie was in the kitchen giving Doris's dress a little touch-up with the iron, Doris sat in the living room looking through Sister Carrie's photo albums and scrapbooks for the zillionth time.

"Sister Carrie?" Doris called out. "Why did you quit show business?"

"Well, I think show business quit me first."

"How do you mean?"

"Let me see. . . . How can I explain it?" Sister Carrie said as she moved out of the kitchen and headed for the spare room with the dress in hand. When she returned, she joined Doris on the couch.

"Well, I was performing at a club in Baltimore. Nice place. Nice money, too. . . . I was backstage touching up my makeup when for the first time in a long time I took a good look at myself, and do you know what I saw?"

"Glory?" Doris teased, because whenever she was in her Sunday best, Sister Carrie often told her she looked like a glimpse of glory.

"No. Not this time," Sister Carrie replied with a speck of sadness in her voice. "What I saw was a woman dressed to the teeth, looking as fabulous as all get-out, but underneath all that . . . a woman with no joy."

"No joy?" Doris questioned. "But you had fancy clothes and you got to travel and you were singing — "

"That's true. But in those days, there was one thing I loved more than singing."

"What?"

"Proving my parents wrong."

Doris gave Sister Carrie a puzzled look.

"You see, when I told my parents I wanted to be a singer, my mother laughed and my father told me to go outside and get a switch. I had whelps all over my legs for days. When I got through sulking, I made up my mind to run away. Two months later, lanky as a reed and almost sixteen, I ran off with — well, that's another story. Anyway, I left for Chicago and started singing with — "

"I know! The Carolina Quartet."

"That's right. . . . The going was sho' nuf rough in the beginning, but I refused to throw in the towel. In those days, Pride was my middle name. And when I was able to start sending money back home to my folks, I was just busting with pride. But I wasn't really sending the money out of pure love. Tucked inside of my outward act of generosity was a hard, cold nugget of spite-work. Every time they got a letter and some dollar bills from me from St. Louis, Chicago, New Orleans, or someplace else around the country, I knew my mama and daddy would have to admit they'd been wrong and I had been right. That I had won."

Sister Carrie paused for a moment.

"That night in Baltimore I had to ask myself what exactly had I won, if when all was said and done, I had no joy, no peace. I felt real . . . empty. Odd thing is, I may have given the best performance of my career that night. I sang hard, trying to sing myself into some joy. But, when I left the club that night, I still felt empty. . . . I had another feeling, too." Sister Carrie paused again, stroking the arm of the couch. "Some other part of me wanted to get a chance to come out. You see, Doris, it's very important to see something up ahead for yourself, to set a course instead of just drifting with the tide. And important as it is to follow your dream, it's more important to follow it for the right reason. Otherwise, at some point down the line — might not be right away — but at some point, it'll dry up on you."

"You couldn't find a right reason to sing?"

"At that point, no . . . A month or so later, I called your mama up. I told her how I was feeling and she talked me into making a visit to New York. When I met your daddy I said to myself, 'Geraldine is one lucky woman.' First time I heard him preach I thought, 'This man is for real. He's truly a man of God.' That night I decided to stay in New York and join Mt. Calvary. The congregation was pretty small back then. But your mama and daddy had high hopes and great expectations. Truth be told, the choir was kind of sorry. They were sincere, but most times their voices missed the mark. Your mama asked me to sing one Sunday — "

"Where was I?"

"You were a little butterball in your mama's stomach and a dream coming true in your daddy's heart. . . . Anyway, I sang that Sunday and the Sunday after that. Before long, word got out that I was singing at Mt. Calvary. Week after week I kept on singing; week after week the pews kept on filling up. Next thing I knew, I had joy and Mt. Calvary was growing strong. I'll never forget the look on your daddy's face that October Sunday morning when the church was packed for the first time. My singing may have drawn a lot of folks in, but it was your daddy's preaching and his leadership that made them stay."

"I miss my daddy," said Doris. "Sometimes it's worse than other times. It'll just creep up on me, like out of nowhere."

"You don't ever stop missing somebody you love."

"I'm always wondering what it would be like if he was still here . . . the kinds of things we'd be doing together. . . ." Doris's voice trailed off into a pause. Then she asked with a frown, "About what you were saying earlier about having no joy. . . . Are you saying that if you sing but it's not church songs, you can't have any joy?"

"No, I'm not saying that at all." Sister Carrie knew by the tone of Doris's voice that there was something more to her question, but she couldn't tell what. "Why'd you ask?"

"Oh, I don't know. It's just that sometimes when I'm at Toni's house and Mrs. Barnett's friends are there and I hear them downstairs singing, and sometimes when I'm looking through your scrapbooks and photographs, I get a feeling like I . . . . Well, I was just wondering if you ever want to go back to singing the blues?"

"Not really. Sometimes I might get the itch, particularly when an old friend is performing in New York and I go to take in their show. Now, I'm sure the Mt. Calvary busybody committee wouldn't take too kindly to that, but I don't see the harm in it. Besides, sometimes I get ideas I can use when I sing in church. After all, gospel and the blues are like first cousins. If you forget about the words, and just listen to the music and the way the voices move through it, you can easily see the family resemblance."

"Brother Wesley once told me that a lot of the music we sing in the church and the stuff folks sing outside of the church are just different branches of the same tree. He said the Spirituals we invented in slavery are the tree trunk. And he said the roots of the tree go all the way back to Africa," Doris said.

"Well, if anyone should know about all the specifics, Brother Wesley should," Sister Carrie said with a laugh. "And you know what we should be doing right now?"

"What?"

"Getting our beauty rest, so we can be bright and shining for the Lord tomorrow morning."

Nine

If spending time with Toni and Sister Carrie was like taking a short vacation in paradise, school was often like being stranded on a desert island — in a part of the world where the sun don't shine. Doris turned in her homework assignments neatly, completely, and on time. She did just what the teachers required. Never, ever did she volunteer to do anything for extra credit. Doris had mastered the art of participating in class just enough to make her teachers think they had her undivided attention, but in reality she usually only listened to them with one ear. In the other ear she reviewed what she had learned at her last piano lesson, ran through the songs the choir was to sing that coming Sunday, and diddled around with her own little tunes. Whenever a song came to her, she jotted the lyrics down in the back of her notebook. When she reached home, she transferred them into her diary. She hadn't forgotten her father's words: "You've got to catch those songs when they come, Doris. Songs have a mind of their own, you know."

So now, along with entries on the happenings and non-happenings in her life, Doris had a growing collection of lyrics, ideas for songs, ideas for titles of songs. Sometimes whole songs — title and all — popped into her head and out onto paper in one fell swoop.

September 24, 1949

I'm going to ride on the wings of a dove,
And Sing for my Creator who lives up above.

Sometimes Doris even wrote about the ones that got away.

December 18, 1949

Dear Diary,

Last night just as I was falling asleep, I got an idea for a song. I remember thinking the title should be "Ring of Glory, Ring of Light."

I should have gotten up and written down the lines that came to me. I thought I would remember them today, but I don't. Maybe someday they'll come back to me.

By now Doris was on another diary. This one was navy blue and larger than the others. The one Sister Carrie gave Doris for her fifteenth birthday was covered in burgundy quilted leather.

January 6, 1950

Dear Diary,

Well, hello there, and how do you do?"

February 3, 1950

Dear Diary,

Wrote two songs and three poems today. I don't know where they come from. They just pop into my mind.

September 13, 1950

Dear Diary,

Toni came over this afternoon. She was on her way to Micheaux's Bookstore and she stopped by to see if I wanted to come with her. She was quiet most of the time we were in the store. And this is the first time I've been in a bookstore with her when she didn't buy a single book. She came back over here with me and stayed a while. When I asked her what was wrong she said, nothing, then a few minutes later she burst into tears. She found out this morning that one of her father's brother's was killed in Korea. A lot of people at Mt. Calvary have friends and family fighting in the war. I just don't get it. I wonder if there really will come a day when it'll be like that passage in Isaiah Daddy used to quote a lot about the day of the Lord: "They shall beat their swords into plowshares, and their spears into pruning-

*hooks, nation shall not lift up sword against
nation, neither shall they learn war any more."*

January 8, 1951

Dear Diary,

*Guess what? Remember I told you that last
week Mrs. King who lives down the block
asked Mama if I ever did any baby-sitting and
Mama said I hadn't but she didn't see any reason I couldn't start to do a little bit. Well, it
looks like I'm going to be doing a lot more than
a little bit. As you know Mrs. King said I did a
very good job and I was very responsible. Well
Mrs. Carter from around the corner just called
and said she needs a baby-sitter for tomorrow
and that Mrs. King had recommended me. This
is great because I could really use the money.*

One week later Mrs. Carter recommended Doris
to Mrs. Reed, who recommended her to Mrs. Wright.
Before long, Doris had a thriving little business. And
she did indeed need the money. Doris took her
singing very seriously and she wanted to have all
the tools of her craft. She couldn't afford everything
she wanted but, before long, she had a pitch pipe,
a metronome, a music stand, and a growing collection of piano and songbooks. Although it was
one of the least expensive things she bought, her
prized possession was the composition book where
she now kept her songs and had, in fact, labeled
"My Songs." When she went for piano lessons, she
showed her songs to the Minister of Music. He cri-

tiqued them and helped her with the music. Occasionally Doris performed some of her songs at the recitals she was now giving at Mt. Calvary and other churches around town.

By now, while no one would call Doris "Stringbean," never again would anyone call her pudgy. Her pigtails were long gone, and she was going to Sister Carrie's shop every other week for a press and curl. Naturally, only Sister Carrie could touch her head; and Sister Carrie treated Doris to the same special shampoos and conditioners she used herself. Doris often coaxed Sister Carrie into giving her one of the hairstyles she'd seen in a magazine, just for fun.

"My, my, my. Ain't you looking free, fine, and almost twenty-one," Sister Carrie sometimes teased. Then she put Doris's hair into a style that Geraldine would think more appropriate for the sixteen-year-old that Doris was.

Doris was often confused about what it meant to be sixteen. Her body signaled her that she would soon be a woman, but her insides sometimes nudged her to retreat back to childhood. Adults didn't make it any easier. They didn't seem to know whether she was a child or a woman either. Sometimes Geraldine would scoop her up in a cuddle of tickles and hugs and ask, "How's my little baby girl doing today?" Thirty minutes later she might stun Doris with, "Now that you're becoming a young lady, it's time you started . . . ," or "Doris, you're not a child anymore. You should know better than that." Then, before the week was out, Doris might find herself confronted with, "Doris, don't come around

here with those womanish ways," or "You're a long
way from grown, my dear."

As Doris walked the tightrope of adolescence, her
body continued to change and her mind continued
to expand. And so did her musical interests and
imagination.

As far as the music of the church was concerned,
the thrill wasn't completely gone, but it was up
against some heavy competition, because a different sound had captivated Doris's ear, mind, and
heart. It was what the churchfolk called "worldly
music." Doris spent hours and hours in her room
alone with her radio, listening to the songs of
women for whom love is bad, sad, full of hurt, re-
jection, and infidelity. In her mind she began to
experience the pain of love, the blues of love, the
hurts of love. Sometimes she fantasized about what
it would be like to experience the joys of romantic
love.

Hour upon hour, she breathed in the sounds of
Dinah Washington, Lena Horne, Sarah Vaughn, Billie Holliday. Late at night she played the songs over
and over again in her head. She sometimes jumped
from song to song, making for an eerie medley. She
leapt from:

> *This bitter earth,*
> *What fruit it bears . . .*

To:

> *Don't know why,*
> *There's no sun up in the sky,*
> *Stormy weather . . .*

To:

> *In my solitude, you haunt me,*
> *With memories of days gone by . . .*

Then to her all-time favorite:

> *Them that's got shall get,*
> *Them that's not shall lose,*
> *So the Bible says*
> *And it still is news,*
> *Mama may have, Papa may have,*
> *But God bless the child that's got his own. . . .*

Doris rolled the songs around in her imagination. She daydreamed about the lives these singers led, longing to see more of the world, yearning to be more a part of it.

"Doris!"

She didn't know the details of her mother's day, but she could tell by the tone of her voice that her mother wasn't in the best of moods. She knew she had better get a smile on her face and a syrupy sweet "Yes, Mama?" on the tip of her tongue by the time Geraldine reached her bedroom door.

"Doris, this morning I told you I'd be a little late tonight. And I asked you to please set the table and heat up the food."

"Sorry, Mama. I was just getting ready to do it, right after I finished my homework."

"It's almost eight o'clock. Since when does it take you all this time to do your homework? Or were you listening to that radio all afternoon?"

"Mama, I only had it on for — "

"Girl, don't fool with me. Think about what you 'bout to say. Think real hard, because I am in no mood . . ."

It had happened before that, so engrossed in the radio, Doris had lost track of time, and Geraldine was halfway up the stairs before Doris could scramble up to turn off the radio and get a book — any book — in front of her face. If her mother had had one of those "rough ones," Doris knew she'd better not push her luck. And so . . . she shut up.

"Doris, when Carrie bought you that radio, my first mind told me to ask her to take it back and get you something else, because I was worried that it might just become a stumbling block."

"But, Mama — "

"Doris! Don't interrupt me! Now, as I was saying . . . we may be in this world, but as they say, we're not to be 'of the world.' And I think, young lady, you're getting just a little too wrapped up in this — this worldly music."

Here we go again, Doris moaned to herself.

March 18, 1951

Dear Diary,

    I got another lecture tonight about being "in" the world, but not "of" it. What on earth does that mean, anyway? I know the world has its problems, but it's where we have to be for the time being so why not enjoy it, right? And what's so wrong with "worldly" music. The songs we sing in church are okay, but they don't cover everything. Like those songs about the storm clouds passing over, and about making it through the darkness, well, those songs sure don't always bring me comfort when I need it. Like the day I waited two hours for Sammy Stone at the library. Two whole hours. And what do I see on my way home but him sitting up in Millie's Luncheonette drinking a milk shake and giving Melinda Brooks goo-goo eyes. And I know one thing for sure. It was Betty Copeland's "That Man's a Fool" that helped me stop crying and get over Sammy Stone. It sure wasn't "Victory in Jesus."

I just don't get it. Music is music. The Bible says that the earth is the Lord's and the fullness thereof. So isn't all the music His? I don't understand what Mama's problem is with "worldly" music. All I know is that she's having a lot of trouble understanding me these days.

In her search for understanding, Doris soon found Berry Hopkins, a rail-thin girl with a lot of teeth who never ceased to amaze Doris with the way she could lie. It was a skill she had been able to cultivate largely because she had so much freedom and free time. When Berry was five, her mother ran off with an insurance agent and she was left to be raised (with the occasional help of two doting aunts) by

her father, Deacon Hopkins, who worked two jobs
Monday through Saturday and slept during service
on Sunday. Doris and Berry had known each other
ever since they were children, but they became fast
friends on the night of the Tenth Annual Young People's Jubilee Concert when they discovered they had
a mutual interest.

The concert was over. The participants were
downstairs in the cafeteria eating ice cream and
cake and swapping their grab-bag prizes. Berry had
won second prize for a very robust rendition of "Go
Down, Moses." Doris had given a steady but rather
lackluster performance of "Revive Us Again." Last
year she had won first prize, but this year she hadn't
even wanted to win. She wouldn't have even entered
the contest had it not been for Geraldine's prodding
and fussing.

Now that it was over, Doris was relieved but still
annoyed that she had had to enter it in the first
place. She sat at one of the tables watching her
scoop of strawberry ice cream melt and wishing she
could be someplace else. Berry, seated across from
her, muttered to no one in particular, "Boy, I'm glad
that's over!"

"Got that right," Doris half grunted.

"I thought you were really into these things,
Doris."

"Used to be," she shrugged. "Not anymore. But
I'm sure I'll be up there again next year if my mother
has anything to do with it. Your father make you
enter?"

"Not really," Berry smirked as she leaned in toward Doris. "See, he's been throwing a lot of hellfire-

and-brimstone talk at me lately. Says I'm straying from the Lord and I need to get more involved in the church. It all started when I asked him for a record player for my birthday, and, well, didn't he go into a tailspin about the evils of worldly music."

"What's with them?" Doris asked.

"Anyway, I figure, I'll start going to church a little more, enter this thing to get him off my back, and get my record player. Then I'll ask him to get me a few, you know, holy records. When he's around I'll throw on some Mahalia Jackson or something. But when he's out of sight and out of mind, it'll be time for some Sam Cooke, Fats Domino, Ruth Brown, Nat King Cole, and — "

"You know, Nat King Cole played the piano for me once when I was singing at my friend Toni's house, only I didn't realize who he was! Now I could just kick myself!"

"Wow! So you didn't get an autograph or anything? That's too bad. You know, I have every single one of his records," Berry boasted.

"But how do you have records if you don't have a player?"

"My friend DeeDee, who lives across the street from me, has one. Her mother's really cool and lets us play whatever we want, when we want. And DeeDee's got even more records than me. You know Bobby's on 125th Street?"

"Yeah."

"Well, DeeDee's mother's friend is a friend of the owner. So she gets googobs of records. Sometimes she gives me her dupes."

"I sure envy you," Doris sighed. "I don't have *any*

records, not to mention a record player," she added as she looked down at the pink puddle on her plate.

Three weeks later Deacon Hopkins presented Berry with an RCA Victor automatic phonograph for her birthday, and half a dozen records by Mahalia Jackson, Clara Ward, Albertina Walker, and other gospel greats. The next day Berry called up Doris to brag.

Doris developed a course of action. She would head out the door on her way to school with her arms filled with books, and Geraldine would smile and sigh. "Well, well, well. Looks like my baby girl is becoming a little scholar." Doris would leave the house with a chipper "See ya later" and a "By the way, Mama, I won't be straight home after school. I need to go to the library." Once in a while Doris actually did go to the library, but nine times out of ten, she was at Berry's house.

In addition to having a phonograph and a great collection of records, Berry had a stack of photographs of singers and musicians. She also had shoe boxes of jewelry and makeup and several pairs of high-heeled shoes, stretch pants, halter tops, muu-muus, and other forbidden goodies she sneaked into when she tiptoed out to dances or the rent parties DeeDee's mother threw on Saturday nights.

When Doris went over to Berry's, DeeDee and her friend Gail were usually there. DeeDee was a small, wiry girl who popped gum incessantly. Her friend Gail was a tall strapping girl with hazel eyes and sandy hair who acted like the baby of the family that she was.

Doris, Berry, DeeDee, and Gail whiled away the hours, dressing up in Berry's clothes, putting on makeup, and lip-syncing to records and songs on the radio. Sometimes they picked a song they all knew backward and forward and created their own version of it. A few times they absolutely butchered a song, but most times — with a change of tempo here, a little improvisation on the lyrics there — they gave an old song a whole new twist. Now and then, Doris tested out one of her own songs on the group. These days, more and more songs were popping into her head and onto the pages of her composition book. But these songs had absolutely nothing to do with her Creator "who lives up above."

When the girls weren't singing, they were fantasizing about what they would or would not do if they had their own singing group. They tried to outdo one another with tales of the lives they'd lead if they were very famous and very rich. Here DeeDee and Berry always had the advantage. DeeDee worked as an usher at the Apollo Theatre a few times a week; Berry sometimes subbed for her. They made Doris and Gail's mouths water with stories about what the stars were like, flaunting the autographs they'd gotten from those who graced the stage and those who came to take in the shows.

With the Apollo Theatre only a block away from her house, Doris had passed by it hundreds of times in her life. But the closest she ever came to the inside of the Apollo was on Wednesday nights when WMCA broadcast Amateur Night at the Apollo. The volume was turned down so low she had trouble hearing everything. But she heard enough to know

that there were young people like herself on stage
live at the Apollo, dancing, singing, and showing
off their talents before a real live audience. As she
lay in bed she tried to imagine what they looked
like, how they moved, what they felt when the audience applauded, and how they stood it when the
audience began to boo and they were shooed
offstage.

"It's just not fair," she sighed as she drifted off to
sleep one night. "Berry and DeeDee get to work at
the Apollo while I'm burping babies."

Doris wasn't really all that frustrated over her
baby-sitting jobs. Very few of the children were
brats. She liked playing the role of 'I'm-the-one-in-
charge', and she, of course, loved the money. And
best of all, some of the people she worked for had
a television set — something Geraldine wanted no
part of. Like many churchfolk, she halfway sus-
pected that the Devil was behind this so-called sign
of progress. She was convinced that television
would only serve to keep people home from church,
and poison their minds — especially young minds.
Doris, of course, disagreed. And she soaked up as
much television as she could when she was baby-
sitting. Her favorite shows were the talent and variety
shows. Some evenings Doris and Berry watched
television together over the phone.

More and more these days when Geraldine looked
at Doris, she didn't like a lot of what she saw. She
had gotten a whiff too many of some rather womanish ways from Doris, and she was also becoming
concerned with the company Doris was keeping.
Geraldine had always thought Toni a bit odd, but

at least she didn't seem dangerous; and Berry was, of course, always her angel-self in front of Geraldine. It was the "other two" that worried Geraldine. The few times they came to the house, DeeDee and Gail didn't know any better than to be themselves. And Geraldine quickly labeled DeeDee "the fast and fresh one," and Gail, "the silly fool."

Geraldine knew you sometimes had to let girls be girls, but she was getting tired of telling Doris to turn the radio either down or off, and tired of worrying about the kind of influence "the other two" might have on her daughter. When Geraldine thought about the summer coming and all the free time Doris would have on her hands, she knew her worries might only increase. Her suspicions were confirmed when she came home early one evening from a church officers' meeting and heard a bluesy tune flowing from her parlor window and also heard Doris scatting and do-wopping away on what Geraldine immediately labeled "some gutter song."

Geraldine rushed up the front steps and into the parlor. "*Girl*, have you lost your mind!"

Doris knew she'd been busted and that there was no squirming around it.

"What kind of foolishness is this?" Geraldine continued; and she went on and on and on and . . . on. Her closing remarks were: "If you think I'm going to put up with this kind of behavior, baby girl, you got another thing coming!"

A few days later Doris found out exactly what that other thing was that was coming.

"Down South!" Doris shrieked.

"Who you raising your voice at, young lady?"

"Sorry, Mama, but — but, Mama, why you gonna make me spend the whole summer down South?"

"Because, missy, I think it would be a good idea for you to get out of the city, and get some fresh country air. Like I told you the other night, you been flying a little too high for my liking, and it's time for me to clip your wings, and put a little distance between you and those two little pieces of trash you and Berry been hanging around."

Ten

June 28, 1951

Dear Diary,

This is my third day in West Point, Virginia.
Ugh! This place is the pits. And I've got another
whole month and a half of these slow-talking,
old-timey, fat-back eating country folks. And
Cousin Larry just can't wait to take me to see
some stupid farm. He's such a dufus! Tomorrow they're throwing me a Welcome to West
Point party. Whoop-de-doo! Oh, God, forgive
me for being so mean but I just hate it down
here.

June 29, 1951

Dear Diary,

Guess who came to the party? Remember Michael? That's right! He's gotten even cuter and he's looking like a real man. Oh, Mama, thank you for sending me to West Point, Virginia!

When Doris was invited to sing at her aunt's church she agreed, of course, only if Michael accompanied her on the piano. Doris saw Michael almost every day. She took to his shy, quiet ways, and she soon began toning down the bit of city-slick in hers. They sometimes went for long walks and had picnics for two. But mostly they sat in Aunt Francine's living room making music. Michael was impressed by how well Doris played the piano. Doris was amazed by how his playing far surpassed her own. She told him she thought he was a musical genius. He told her her voice was an inspiration. Together, they wrote songs.

The days skipped by, and before Doris knew it, August was tomorrow. And Geraldine came down to visit for a week with her family and take Doris home. Geraldine's sister had, of course, told her about Michael. But since Francine had also given Doris an A+ for attitude and behavior during the summer, Geraldine wasn't too upset about a little puppy love. And after she met Michael she wasn't worried at all. For she quickly labeled him "a nice, mannerable, churchgoing boy."

The night before she left for home, Doris and

Michael sat out on the porch whispering about how much fun they had had together. She kept waiting to hear him say those marvelous, magical, melodious words: "I love you." Those words never came from Michael's lips, but Doris heard them in the flow of his voice as he said, "I'll write." She felt them when he kissed her on the cheek and let his hands rest briefly on her waist before he said, "Good-bye." At that point Doris no longer needed to hear those magical words. She knew that shy types didn't always say in words what they meant. And as Michael stepped down from the porch, she began to think it wouldn't be such a bad idea to one day live in West Point, Virginia.

Doris came home with a heart full of love. And a lot to tell her friends. The first person she told about Michael was Toni, who quickly talked her into imagining her and Michael one day working together as a musical team. When Doris got together with Berry, DeeDee, and Gail, her romance really began to take on epic proportions. When they pressed her for all the details, Doris didn't exactly lie, she just stretched the truth a little. And when they double-dared her to be the first to write, she met the challenge. And Michael soon wrote back. In that letter and in the ones to come, Michael never said the magical words. But Doris felt she knew his heart, and with a little help from her friends she felt she was becoming an expert at reading between the lines.

Doris was soon back into her usual routine. In school, she did only what she had to do. She only went to church when she had to. Several times a week she was again going to the "library," and she was back on the market as a baby-sitter. Doris was smarter about things this time around: she never let the names of "the other two" slip from her lips. She made sure that Geraldine only caught her practicing "holy music" on the piano, and in every way acted like the God-fearing daughter she knew her mother wanted to see.

One evening when Doris was baby-sitting for the Carters, she called Berry up to remind her that one of their favorite shows was coming on. But before she could finish saying, "Hi, it's me," Berry jumped in with, "Can't talk to you right now. Gotta call DeeDee back and tell her I can't find anybody to — wait a minute! What are you doing on Friday night?"

"Nothing. Why?"

"DeeDee's gotta go to a funeral and she needs somebody to sub for her at the Apollo. I can't do it because Aunt Thelma and Aunt Trudy are coming over. You think you can do it? Come on, say you'll do it." After a pause she teased, "You might get some great autographs."

"But my mother — ooh, that's right! Friday nights she's at all-night prayer service. Berry, tell DeeDee I can do it!"

That Friday, when Doris made her way through the glass outer doors of the world-famous Apollo Theatre, she was all but flying. She reported to the supervisor and then changed into her uniform in a flash because she didn't want to waste any time being any place other than inside the auditorium.

With her excitement overflowing, Doris was super-
usher that night: super-polite, super-alert, super-
quick. And she was super-delighted whenever she
got a ticket holder with orchestra seats, because it
gave her a chance to walk that much closer to the
stage and also get a wide-angle view of the thea-
ter — from the gallery high above to the balcony
below it and on down to the lower mezzanines, then
back up to the loges on either side that stair-stepped
toward the stage. In the hubbub of the crowd she
heard raw energy; in the glint and gleam of the lights
she saw glory; and in the very air she breathed, Doris
smelled wonder. The Apollo filled her with a sense
of awe that until now she had felt only inside a
church sanctuary.

At one point, as Doris was escorting a man down
to his seat in the orchestra section, she fell into a
panic when she spotted the back of a head that
looked like it belonged to a woman who lived on
her block and knew her mother well. When the
woman turned to her companion, Doris knew from
the profile that she had been mistaken, but she
nevertheless remained uneasy. This uneasiness
split off into a knot of fear and a spasm of guilt. As
Doris walked back up the aisle to her post, she
wrestled with these feelings. But in the end, the
energy, the glory, and the wonder of the Apollo won
out. Doris made peace with her deceit and her dis-
obedience, convinced that this was where she
needed to be, that this was something she just had
to do. And she also decided then and there that if
given the opportunity she would do it again.

As it turned out, Doris subbed several more times

for DeeDee and a few other ushers. And all the while Geraldine was on her knees before the altar, thanking God for such a studious and God-fearing daughter.

It was one thing to see the stars live on stage. But once Doris became more fearless and began going backstage, it was another thing altogether to see Billie Holiday, Pearl Bailey, Sam Cooke, and so many other great singers up so close and in person. One night as the inimitable Sarah Vaughn headed to her dressing room with a trail of applause behind her, she said to Doris: "So how did I sound, bright eyes?"

"Oh, ma'am, you were wonderful." Doris beamed. "I wish I could sing as beautiful as you."

"What's your name, darlin'?"

"Doris Winter, ma'am."

"Can you sing, Miss Doris Winter?"

"Yes."

"Well, let me hear a little something."

Doris sang a few lines of "Blue Moon," then dropped her head slightly.

"Well! I'll be! Looks like I'm going to have some pretty stiff competition in a few years," said Sarah Vaughn, but she was only half teasing.

Doris was in seventh heaven because these days, though she wasn't exactly dreaming of singing for the whole wide world, she was dreaming hard about singing for a bigger world than the church choir circuit. And the more contact she had with the performers at the Apollo, the more her dream took root.

Doris seized every opportunity to be around the performers, and her motivation was about more than mere stargazing. Just as she studied their vocal techniques, and their onstage mannerisms and moves, she also studied their offstage behavior and deportment. She was able to observe the nitty-gritty of the entertainment business. And sometimes she saw things that weren't so pretty: like which great talents were anything but great human beings. For those who won her admiration as both performers and people, Doris jumped at the chance to do any little bit of scut work they might ask of her. And even in running a simple errand, she felt there was something to be learned. Sometimes the performers sent her out for a soda, a cup of coffee, or something to eat. Doris would shoot over to Chock Full O'Nuts on Seventh Avenue or Teddy's Shanty on Eighth and return lickety-split with extra napkins and never a mistake as to who had ordered the black coffee, who wanted it regular, who wanted ketchup on their French fries and who wanted them plain. To her surprise, she made more money from tips than she did from ushering. And these days, she really needed the money.

Doris's wants were getting more expensive, and many of them were only loosely related to her craft. Every week or so she bought herself a little something and stashed it away in a coat box hidden under her bed behind her suitcases. Before long, the box was full of treasures: nail polish, rouge, eyeliner, a pair of false eyelashes, a few pairs of stockings, and some costume jewelry. She also had a few scarves, handkerchiefs, and sashes she made from fabric Mrs. Barnett gave her. Doris's prized possession was a pair of black high-heeled shoes.

Evenings when Geraldine was at church, Doris turned on her radio, pulled out her treasure chest, and transformed herself into a star. Her lips became flamingo red; her cheekbones, a swatch of deep rose. She'd fling a long scarf around her neck, tie a sash around her waist. She strolled, sauntered, and switched around her room in her three-inch heels. She'd strike poses in her doorway, trying hard to look as sultry as Dorothy Dandridge or Hazel Scott. She purred like Eartha Kitt. Sometimes she stood before the mirror and did a little bump and grind. Then she'd stand straight and tall — right foot pointed out, hands on her hips, chin up, cheeks sucked in — batting her eyelashes away.

Doris was poised just so one crisp, cool October evening, and she was loving every inch of herself. In fact, all day Doris had been feeling free, frisky, and fantastic! Free enough to say yes when DeeDee asked her to sub for her that night. Frisky enough to tell her mother Mrs. Carter was desperate for a baby-sitter. And now that Geraldine had gone to visit a sick friend, Doris felt fantastic enough to leave the house all dolled up — rhinestone-studded hair-clips, high-heeled shoes, and all.

On the way to the Apollo, Doris wobbled only twice. Both times, she recovered very quickly, very gracefully.

When Doris entered the Apollo, the staff manager did a double take and looked her up and down for a long minute. Then, with a wink and a nod, he called her over. "Hey, good lookin', would ya like to be head usher tonight and take the tickets?"

"I'd be delighted," Doris replied with a bat of her eyes. "Thank you, Mark," she added as she sashayed away to change into her uniform.

While Doris was in the lobby of the Apollo Theatre taking tickets — still feeling free, frisky, and fantastic — Charlotte Caine was lumbering down 125th Street.

As usual, Charlotte Caine was minding what should have been God's business. Based on their appearances, she picked out who among the passersby were saints, and who among them were sinners. And she knew for sure that those entering the Apollo would be at the top of the list of sinners. So when Charlotte Caine reached the Apollo's marquee, she stopped and snarled, "Sinners!" With a sidelong glance she added, "God's watching!" Her sidelong glance turned into a bold-faced stare. Then step by step, it became a squinch-eyed peer through the Apollo's glass outer doors.

Geraldine was out on her front stoop chatting with a few neighbors when Charlotte Caine huffed and puffed down the block, like a wolf ready for the kill.

"Evenin', Sister Caine," Geraldine said as the wolf neared her house.

"Praise God, everybody! Sorry to be the bearer of bad news, Sister Winter, but your daughter is poised on the brink of Hell!"

"Beg pardon?"

"That's right," Charlotte Caine continued between huffs and puffs. "Seen her with my own eyes, roun' the corner there at the Apollo thee-*ater*."

"Beg pardon," Geraldine repeated. "Doris at the Apollo? With all due respect, you must be mistaken. Doris is baby-sitting for the Carters tonight."

"Not unless they done moved into the Apollo thee-*ater*, she ain't. Seen her standing right there in the lobby, lookin' right hussy-ish, if truth be told. She was taking the people's tickets, smilin' at all the mens, and everythin'."

"Sister Caine, are you sure it was Doris? *My* Doris?"

"Uh-huh, as God is my witness. If you don't b'lieve me — "

Geraldine charged upstairs. She grabbed her hat from the foot of her bed, and snatched her pocketbook off the dresser. She needed neither. But Geraldine Winter never left home without a hat on her head or a pocketbook on her arm.

"Be glad to come and show you right where she is," grinned Charlotte Caine as Geraldine charged down the front steps.

"Thank you, Sister Caine," Geraldine said tersely. "But I know precisely where the Apollo is, and full well what my daughter looks like."

Doris felt a tingle skitter up her spine. She felt eyes roaming up and down her body. Mark's at it again, she said to herself. With a little wiggle of her hips she shifted from one foot to the other. Guess there's no harm in his looking, she thought.

"Well, I'll be!" seethed Geraldine as she stared with unbelieving eyes through the Apollo's glass outer doors.

The tingle was crawling up Doris's spine again. This time it was followed by a hot breath on her neck and a firm grip that spun her around into —

"Mama!"

"What in the h — world are you doing here!" Geraldine's rage had boiled over. Her voice was raised to the hilt.

The people in the lobby were all ears. All eyes. Mark looked Geraldine up and down and decided he had better stay out of this one.

"Mama, I — "

Geraldine grabbed Doris by the hand. Doris pulled away. For a split second, it looked as if Doris's hand was poised for a slap. An instant later, Doris lowered her arm, but she raised her voice slightly.

"Mama, please, you're embarrassing me."

"*I'm* embarrassing *you!*"

With each word, Geraldine gave Doris a poke in the chest. With each poke, Doris wobbled a step backward. By now her back was up against a wall. She cringed at the sight of all the people in the lobby. Gawking. Murmuring. Snickering.

"Look at you all gussied up like some woman twice your age with half your sense! And in a place like this!"

"But, Mama, I want to be a singer, a real singer, and this is where I have to be if I'm going to learn anything."

"*Girl!* Don't you know that road is paved with nothing but temptations?"

"But — "

Geraldine grabbed Doris's arm again. This time Geraldine's grip was an iron claw. Without another word, she wrenched Doris forward.

"But, Mama, I want to sing," Doris whimpered as Geraldine yanked her through the lobby and out the doors of the Apollo Theatre.

"But, Mama, I want to sing," Doris stammered as Geraldine dragged her down 125th Street.

Geraldine showed no mercy. Each time Doris wobbled in her high-heeled shoes, Geraldine only yanked her harder. Doris recovered neither quickly nor gracefully. A few steps behind, Sister Caine kept on shouting at the top of her voice, "Who woulda believed it! Who woulda believed it!"

Eleven

October 11, 1951

Dear, Dear, Dearest Diary,

How are you tonight? I trust your life isn't as rotten as mine. In case you've forgotten who I am, I'm the girl who can't do anything she wants to do. Can't wear makeup, or stockings, can't go to dances or the really good movies and naturally as Her Highness would say, "I have to be ever mindful of the company I keep." Good guggamugga, Lord knows what'll happen to me if I don't stay away from those worldly people! All because I am the daughter of Saint Geraldine Winter the Holy. And now that I'm on punishment there're a lot more things I can't do. Can't go to Toni or Berry's house, can't have company, can't talk on the phone, and no more baby-sitting. Can't listen to my radio. Can't even

*look at it, either. The dragon lady took it and
said it's going to sit in the bottom of her closet
until she feels I've learned my lesson.*

*I still can't get over it. How could she have
done that to me? In front of all those people.
Slinging me around like that. Yelling like a
crazy person. Talking to me like I don't have
a right to be me.*

Punishment had its benefits, however. For one
thing, Doris put more time and attention into her
homework. Punishment had also given her more
time to think: to dig a little deeper into herself.

As the holidays approached, Geraldine's heart
softened, and after Thanksgiving, bit by bit she gave
Doris back her freedom. First, time with her friends
after school, then phone privileges, then the baby-
sitting. On the evening of her seventeenth birthday
Doris got her radio back.

January 6, 1952

Dear Diary,

Happy birthday to me.
*It rained all day today. But have no fear,
right? "Because God gave Noah the rainbow
sign. Won't be water but fire next time." That's
something to look forward to. But for the past
few days, "Didn't it rain, children!" Talk about
rain! Oh! My! Lord! When it stops I guess we'll
all just "wade in the water." Cause "God's
gonna trouble the water." Whoop-de-doo!*
I wonder what Daddy would say if I told him

I didn't want to just sing in the choir. I wonder if he'd understand that I don't hate the church or anything, but it's just that I got all kinds of music in me. I wonder if he'd understand me any better than Mama. Mama is so afraid I'm going to become fast or something and thinks I'm just some starry-eyed kid. She thinks places like the Apollo are some kind of trap or something. But I learned so much. I got to see a lot, and I could see myself up there on stage. Every time I went to the Apollo, it was like I started believing in myself more and more.

P.S. Michael hasn't answered my last two letters and he didn't even send me a birthday card. Oh, God, if something's happened to him I'll just die.

Two weeks later when Doris came home from school, she knew that she would live when she saw a letter on her bed. Postmark: West Point, Virginia.

"Oh, thank you, Jesus!" Doris shrieked as she ripped open the letter.

"Oh, God! I can't believe it!" she gasped as she read the letter a second time.

"Oh, no, this can't be happening to me," she murmured as she dropped onto her bed and her vision clouded over with tears.

Michael Emmanuel Merriweather had been more confused and lonely than shy. Two weeks before Doris had arrived in West Point, he had broken up with his girlfriend, Sally Sue. Now they were mended, and getting married in the summer. Doris had done too much reading between the lines.

Doris scanned the letter again and read the P.S. three times.

". . . if you're going to be down here, would you do me the honor of singing at my wedding?"

Doris would have probably cried for the rest of the afternoon if the phone hadn't rung.

"Hi, Doris."

"Hi, Toni."

"What's wrong?"

Doris told Toni about everything that was wrong and worked herself back up into a tearful frenzy. Just as she was about to choose to be miserable for the rest of her life, Toni interrupted with, "Doris, remember when we were younger how you sometimes tried to scare me into going to church by telling me about Judgment Day and the signs of the end in the Bible?"

"Yeah," Doris said slowly, very perplexed and the least bit annoyed.

"Well, unless Michael's getting married was on the list, then this can't be the end of the world."

"Oh, Toni!" Doris laughed in spite of herself.

Toni laughed back to encourage a few more giggles from her friend. "So, that being the case . . . why don't you get yourself over here around eight o'clock. Mom's having a little party and it'll be a heavy show biz crowd so I know you're gonna love it."

"I'll have to ask my mother. I'm still on probation, you know."

"Well, if she says yes, get her to let you sleep

over. I think it's gonna be one of those until-the-wee-hours-of-the-morning affairs."

Doris told Geraldine enough to get her consent, and left home that evening in a simple skirt and blouse and her overnight bag. As soon as she got to Toni's she slipped into her little black dress, her high-heeled shoes, and all the rest.

Doris had never seen the Barnett house this crowded, so crowded in fact that the parlor soon overflowed and the laughter and merriment spilled into the kitchen and the dining room, and flowed up into the family room on the second floor, where people were playing charades, twenty questions, and other party games.

As Doris exchanged glances, smiles, and hand-shakes with dozens of famous and wanna-be famous actors and actresses, dancers and singers, musicians, writers, comedians, and producers, she grew breathless and almost giddy. And it wasn't long before she started to believe that Michael's getting married wasn't the end of the world.

Throughout the evening Doris's eyes roamed the crowd, in vain, in search of the man with the black velvet voice. This time, she thought, I'll be sure to get his autograph. But Doris soon forgot about getting his or anyone else's autograph when someone struck the first chords of "Rhapsody in Blue" and a crowd began to form in the music corner. For the next hour or so, the parlor was nonstop music as this one and that one took a turn at the piano, and as this one and that one called out a request for a song. Through laughter and teasing, and joking and jest, with gusto and rhythm and bravado and zest,

the impromptu choir of strangers and friends ca-
reened through "Old Man River," "A-Tisket, A-Tas-
ket," "Mes Deux Amours," "Minnie the Moocher,"
"Reckless Blues," and some of every other kind of
song.

At one point, there was a noisy lull, when voices
rested and minds searched memory banks for another all-time hit that hadn't been sung. Someone
called out for "Satin Doll," another shouted for
"Stormy Weather." And before Doris knew what
came over her, she let out a soulful, stirring:

> *Them that's got shall get,*
> *Them that's not shall lose . . .*

The noisy lull became a hush. The woman playing
the piano called out, "Hey, now, let whoever it is
through. I don't play for nobody I can't see."

With urgings, nudgings, and friendly prodding,
Doris made her way to the piano. The woman at the
piano quickly found Doris's key and Doris continued
to sing:

> *So the Bible says,*
> *And it still is news.*
> *Mama may have, Papa may have,*
> *But God Bless the child that's got his own. . . .*

Doris barely got through the closing note before
the crowd was cheering and tossing up words of
praise.

"Hey, girl, great set of pipes! . . . Don't let Billie
Holiday hear about how you done stole her song.

. . . Mitch Booker should hear about you. He's looking for a singer for his band. . . . Haven't I seen you at the Savoy? . . ."

Doris was flattered and overwhelmed. She felt like one of the crowd, a woman of the world. Then the next thing she knew, Mrs. Barnett had her arm around her shoulder and was introducing her to everyone.

". . . a friend of Toni's, but we consider her family."

Several in the crowd let out a casual "Oh," and Doris felt like just another schoolgirl again. But then the crowd broke out in another round of cheers and applause and were again tossing up words of praise.

"Like I said, girl, great set of pipes! . . . You still better not let Billie hear about how you . . . Well, she oughta be singing at the Savoy . . ."

From the other end of the room someone shouted out, "Hey, everybody! Dmitri's going to juggle!" As the crowd ebbed away to see Dmitri juggle, Doris remained at the piano dizzy with delight.

"Don't ever let me catch you around any of the places I work," the woman who'd been playing said rather gruffly. Then she added with a smile, "Because, girl, you sho' nuf good!"

"Thank you, ma'am."

"So, you a singer or what?"

"Well, I want to be. I dream about it and — "

"You *dream* about it?! That and a dime will get you to Brooklyn, but it sure won't get you no career. A career ain't no egg, and you ain't no chicken. You got to do something about your dream. They don't just hatch by themselves."

"I want to but I don't know — "

"You live here in Harlem?"

"Yes, ma'am."

"Well, then, shoot, girl, I don't have to tell you. Go on and get yourself up there on stage at Amateur Night at the Apollo one of these Wednesdays. Honey, with a voice like that — "

Before the woman could finish, a young man vaulted over to her with, "Alberta! Alberta! Guess who just arrived?"

Doris didn't hear who had just arrived and she didn't care. The only thing on her mind was what were now for her truly marvelous, magical, melodious words, "Amateur Night at the Apollo."

Doris was still thinking about those magic words in the wee hours of the morning and on into the next day. Her doubts, fears, hopes, and dreams kept clashing and colliding. Inside of Doris, turmoil reigned for a day. Late Saturday evening as she lay in bed, she listened closely and carefully for that still, small voice. When she got home from church on Sunday she telephoned Berry, DeeDee, then Gail. The following afternoon they gathered at Berry's house.

"So, is everyone still ready, willing, and able?" Doris said once the girls were all settled into Berry's bedroom.

"I can see the headlines already!" Berry proclaimed.

"DeeDee?"

"What did I say last night?" DeeDee huffed.

"Honey chile, when DeeDee McKintyre says she's in, she's in."

"Gail?"

"Well . . . after I got off the phone with you, Doris, I started to think, you know, what if my parents find out I'm performing at the Apollo and — "

"And how are they going to find out?" DeeDee snapped back. "Unless you talk in your sleep or — "

"Look, Gail," Berry interrupted. "If we win Amateur Night our parents will *have* to be proud of us, and we'll be so close to famous, they won't have any choice but to take us seriously. And if we lose — "

"If we lose, they'll never even know we entered. And as they say, what they don't know won't hurt them," Doris added soberly. Then she looked Gail in the eye and said, "If you're not up to it, fine. Now's the time to back out."

"I, uh, um — " Gail flubbered. After a pause she added, "Okay, I'm in."

"So, what'll we call ourselves?" DeeDee said between smacks of Juicy Fruit gum.

"Ooh, I got it! The Twilights!" Berry proudly blurted out.

For the next few minutes the girls tossed out a bevy of names: the Satinettes, the Sentinels, the Harbingers of Love, the Velvettes, La Corsage. When this invisible pile of names had almost reached the ceiling, Doris said, "I know exactly what to call ourselves: The Halos."

"The *what!*" DeeDee squawked.

"The Halos," Doris repeated with more conviction in her voice.

"The *Halos!* I don't want to sound like I'm some angel flying around, plucking on some harp or — "

"Wait, DeeDee," Berry jumped in. "I kinda like it. Yeah . . . The Halos. Sounds smooth."

"It's not just that," Doris explained. "It's coming from a different place. Who needs another group that ends with an '-ette.' The Halos is different. Just like we'll be different. Different sound, different everything."

"Yeah," sighed DeeDee. "The Halos. I like it."

"And you know what else?" said Doris, cocking her head to the side and looking up. "It's a way of asking for divine protection."

The other three girls stared at Doris for a moment, trying to catch a glimpse of whatever she was seeing.

Berry, DeeDee, and Gail rolled the name around in their mouths. They moved about the room echoing each other with:

"The Halos."

"The Halos."

"The Halos."

Each time one of them uttered "The Halos," she thrust herself into a pose she thought most glamorous. In the meantime, Doris's mind proceeded to the next item on the agenda.

"Okay. If we're going to win, we're going to have to be the best, right? That means we have to rehearse, and rehearse, and rehearse, and rehearse and . . . rehearse! And when we rehearse, we rehearse. No stopping for phone calls. No stopping for chitchat. No stopping to get anything to eat. No stopping to get anything to drink. No stopping for nothing! Got it?"

Berry, DeeDee, and Gail all got it.

The Halos settled on Thursday afternoons as their rehearsal time. They would still get together other times during the week to pal around, but Thursdays would be serious business. The next item on the agenda was their repertoire. "Why do we need to work on more than one song?" Gail wanted to know. "They only let you do one number, right?"

"Because if we win, in addition to the cash prize, we get a week's engagement at the Apollo," Berry explained.

"And," added Doris, the voice of reason, "we have to act as if we are going to win and be prepared."

Another invisible pile began to mount up to the ceiling. This one was of a slew of the latest songs and a host of oldies-but-goodies. After a few minutes, Doris grew bored with the list.

"For Amateur Night we need to be as original as possible. First of all, it's risky to do a song everybody knows. Unless we do something super-unique and special, people will be bored. And just on GP, we want to be a fresh new package from head to foot."

"She's right," said Berry.

"Hey!" DeeDee said. "What about that song Doris was playing around with a couple of weeks ago?"

"You mean 'Cool Shoes'?"

"No, the one about — "

" 'Me and the Moonlight'?"

"No, the one you wrote when you were all upset about not hearing from Michael."

I will not cry, Doris thought. And this is not the time to tell them about Michael.

" 'Now He's Gone'?" Doris asked calmly, despite the sudden stab of pain she felt.

"Yeah, that's the one!"

"How does it go, again?" Gail wanted to know.

Doris hummed a few bars of the melody and then sang a few verses. She sang it like she meant it. Because she did.

"Yeah, that's our song for Amateur Night!" DeeDee said as she moved to the beat.

The Halos met every week at the appointed day and hour to fine-tune their voices, their moves, their steps. They met mostly at Berry's and occasionally they went to Toni's, where they could have the parlor and the baby grand piano all to themselves because Mrs. Barnett had no problem letting girls be girls. Doris was relentlessly demanding, so much so that a few times Gail collapsed into tears.

"Why do we have to do it again. I thought the first time was quite good."

"Gail, quite good is not good enough."

Doris occasionally let Toni sit in on rehearsals and play audience. Toni took her role very seriously, her mind working overtime about the details.

"Doris?" she asked one day. "Don't you need a tape or something so the band will know what and how to play?"

"No problem. All I have to do is give them the chords, the key, and the beat. They can take it from there. The house band at the Apollo is one of the best."

Toni was always at the ready with her pad and pen, and took great pride in giving the group notes. "DeeDee, you're still making too many faces, and you're shaking your hips too hard. This is not burlesque. . . . Gail, don't stare straight into my eyes all the time. Mix it up a little. You know, look just above my head or past my ear or something." Oftentimes Toni's comments were helpful, but sometimes Doris had to warn Toni that she was overdoing it.

On the last Thursday in April, Toni showed up at Berry's house with three huge shopping bags and a bulging knapsack.

"It's surprise time!" she teased. "But I know, Doris. Rehearsal first. Surprises later."

The rehearsal went exceptionally well. The girls were a unit. Their moves were smooth and crisp. Their voices merged gloriously. At rehearsal's end, Toni hadn't a single note.

"What's the surprise?" Gail immediately asked.

"Okay, everybody, close your eyes," commanded Toni.

After the sound of rustling paper had subsided, Toni told the girls to open their eyes. When they did, they found laid out on Berry's bed four ballet-length violet satin dresses. The dresses had a sweetheart neckline and crinolines sewn into the skirt. Next to each dress lay a shawl made of the same violet lace that covered the bodice of the dress. Beside the bed were four pairs of violet peau de soie pumps with three-inch heels and a thin band of sequins around the top of the shoe.

"Now, because Doris is the lead singer she needs to look a little different," Toni said as she pulled another bag from her knapsack. "So what we can do is glue some of these small sequins on the toes of her shoes, and maybe on the back and the heels, then sew some of these larger ones onto her shawl."

"Can't we have a little more sequins on our shoes, too?" Gail whined.

"Well, okay, but just a little on the toe," Toni gave in.

As the girls went to try on their dresses, Toni went digging into her knapsack again and tossed more packages onto the bed.

"Gloves. Earrings. Bracelets. Some silk flowers for your hair. Some hair combs. Some clips."

"Toni, where on earth did you get all this stuff?" Berry exclaimed.

"My mother was working on some costumes a while ago for a musical, and, well, the producer was a deadbeat. He didn't pay her for the first batch she delivered, so he never got the second batch. At first she was going to sue him, but she decided to let the Fates deal with him. Anyway, when Doris called me up the other day and started talking to me about costumes, I started thinking. She said she wanted The Halos to sound *and* look the best. This was the best I could come up with." Jokingly, and with an exaggerated curtsy, Toni added, "The only question that remains is, is my best good enough for Doris Winter and The Halos."

"Are you kidding, Toni, we love it!" Doris exclaimed as she twirled into a blur of violet. When she spun to a stop, she gave Toni a big hug and a huge, "Thank you very, very much!"

"Oh, I forgot," said Toni as she reached in her

coat pocket for one last remaining bag. "I picked up some paste-on jewelry. Thought you might want to put some on your arms or maybe around your shoulders."

With a flawless rehearsal behind them and exquisite costumes before them, The Halos decided they were ready to audition for Amateur Night at the Apollo. The following Monday, they did just that.

The Halos made it through their audition with a lot of confidence and only a few minor glitches. Gail turned her ankle during one of their shimmy steps, and DeeDee went slightly off-key on one line. Doris had been a bit distracted at first by the glare of the stage lights, but she held tight to her concentration; she held tight to her song.

When it was over, all Doris heard was her heart beating double-time against the backdrop of silence. Then a voice from midway back in the orchestra seats called out, "O.K., kids, you're on this week."

The Halos gasped and squealed with one voice. Doris had an impulse to run down from the stage and smother the invisible stranger with hugs, kisses, and "thank-you-thank-you's." But she restrained herself and only shrieked *"Really?"* as she stepped forward and strained to catch a glimpse of the face behind the voice.

"Yeah, really, honey," the voice responded drily.

"Oh, thank you, thank — "

"Next!" the voice interrupted.

When The Halos exited stage right, they were met by a woman with a clipboard and the question, "The Halos, right?"

"Yes, The Halos," Doris said with the ring of high pride in her voice.

"What's the name of the song you're doing?" the woman asked.

" 'Now He's Gone,' " said Doris.

"Who wrote it?"

"I did. Doris Winter."

" 'Now He's Gone' by Doris Winter," the woman repeated as she wrote it all down.

"That's right," Doris said. But what she thought was: And so am I, Mama, so am I.

Twelve

"**O**hmigod!" Doris shrieked as The Halos stepped outside the Apollo Theatre.

"What?!" the other girls responded in unison.

"Wednesday night is choir rehearsal!"

"But, Doris, this is revival week," Berry reminded her. "And all the regular stuff gets canceled."

"That's right!" Doris said with a sigh of relief.

"And your mother will be in service at least until midnight."

"Yeah, but how do I get out of going to service?"

"Tell her you got a stomachache," suggested DeeDee.

"That won't work. Unless I'm moaning and rolling over the bed, Mama'll just say when I get to church the Holy Spirit will take my mind off the pain."

"What about me?" Gail piped up. "What do I tell my folks?"

"I've got it!" said Berry, "*I'll* have really bad

cramps on Wednesday morning. Besides, I'd like to take the day off and — "

"But, Berry," interrupted DeeDee, "didn't you tell your father you had cramps the other week when you played hooky and went to — "

"He won't remember. Girl, I could — "

"But, Berry, how does that help *me!*" Doris implored.

"And what about me?" whimpered Gail.

"Will you *please* let me finish?" Berry replied, stamping her foot and punctuating the pause with a pompous, "Thank you!"

As Berry laid out the plan, the girls walked to Seventh Avenue.

The plan was a relatively simple one. Sometime between that night and the next, Berry, Gail, and Doris would casually let their parents know that they were having a big history test on Thursday. On Wednesday morning Berry would moan her way into her father's bedroom, complain of a horrendous stomachache, and confess that she didn't think she could make it to school. She would than ask her father to call Geraldine Winter, tell her how sick Berry was, and ask if Doris could bring Berry's homework by and then stay to help her study for the test. If all went according to plan, Deacon Hopkins would also let Geraldine know he was working a double shift and assure her that he would leave Berry money so that she and Doris could get dinner from the luncheonette around the corner. Mr. and Mrs. Sparks were not as rigid as Geraldine, so all Gail had to do was tell her parents she was going over to Berry's house to study and she would be in the clear. DeeDee didn't need a story at all. She could tell her mother she was going to the moon and the most Mrs. McKintyre might say is "Pick me up a bag of barbecue potato chips on your way back."

"So," Berry concluded, "once everybody gets to my house we'll have a dress rehearsal, and then next stop, the Apollo!"

With that, Berry, DeeDee, and Gail headed south on Seventh Avenue. Doris jaywalked across the avenue to 126th Street.

That evening when Geraldine and Doris were halfway through dinner, Doris let it drop that she had a big history test on Thursday.

A few minutes later Geraldine commented, "You know, Doris, you have a strange little glow about you. Matter of fact, there's been something different about you for the past few weeks. That Sammy Stone hasn't been sniffing around you again, has he?"

"Oh, no, Mama."

"Well, like I said, there's something different about you lately."

"It's probably just, you know, spring in the air or something."

"Good Lord," said Geraldine, glancing up at the kitchen clock. "Speaking of spring, we better spring on out of here soon. Evangelist Simmons is preaching tonight. There'll be a crowd for sure."

On Wednesday morning everything went as planned. At breakfast Geraldine told Doris about the call she had received from Deacon Hopkins.

". . . I said that would be fine by me, but I want

you to make sure you're home before eleven o'clock." After a pause she added, "You know, Doris, something here just ain't right."

A piece of toast caught in Doris's throat.

"You and Berry are such good friends, and it just dawned on me that I haven't been very gracious. I should have Berry and Deacon Hopkins over for Sunday dinner sometime. I'm sure they could use every home-cooked meal they can get."

Doris swallowed the piece of toast with ease.

"That's a good idea, Mama" is what Doris said. But in her mind she was saying, Yes, fine, anything. Have them over every Sunday and on Mondays, too! Just let me get out of this house!

"And one more thing," Geraldine said as she made her way to the stove.

What now? wondered Doris.

"I brewed up some red clover tea. Drop it by Berry's on your way to school. It'll help with her stomach."

A few minutes later, just as Doris was almost through the door, Geraldine called out, "Doris, tell Berry to drink a cup of that tea every few hours."

En route to school, Doris poured the red clover tea into the gutter and stuffed the thermos in her schoolbag.

Between 8:45 and 3:15 the clock took twice as long to tick and tock. When the school day was finally over, Doris made a beeline for Berry's house for one last run-through of their act.

Then it was seven o'clock before they knew it. The Halos were backstage at the Apollo Theatre.

For the first time in her life, DeeDee was having

trouble with her lipstick. She kept putting it on, then wiping it off, then applying it again — each time her mouth became more and more ghoulish-looking. At one point, Berry discovered a run in her right stocking; she tried to keep still, hoping it wouldn't reach her calf until after their performance. Out of nowhere, butterflies descended upon Doris. They did a jig and then a tap dance all over her stomach.

Surprisingly, Gail was cool and the only one calm enough to tiptoe forward every now and then to size up the competition.

"They don't have anything on us," she reported of the Debonnaires. "They have some smooth moves. But as you can hear, their singing ain't nothing to write home about."

All Gail said about the Harmonettes was that the lead singer looked stiff, and all the girls had the same amount of sequins on their shoes. Gail never had a chance to observe the young comedian in the gray sharkskin suit. He got as far as "What do you get when you cross a cockroach and a lima bean?" when the audience booed and hissed over the punch line and he was chased off the stage. The audience allowed the tap dance team of ten-year-old Tommy Miller and twelve-year-old Buddy Camp to make it through their act and rewarded the boys with healthy applause. But The Halos were not as worried about them as they were about the Pickett Sisters, who were on next. They had won Amateur Night at the Half-Note three weeks ago.

When Gail came back to report on them, Doris, DeeDee, and Berry peppered her with questions.

"How do their outfits look under the lights?"

"What are their steps like?"

"Could you see the looks on the faces of the audience?"

"Uh, I don't know," was all Gail said.

"What do you mean you don't know!" Berry snapped.

"All I know," replied Gail, "is that I ain't going on. I'm getting out of here."

"WHAT?" the girls said in unison.

"Not going on! What are you talking about? We're on next!" Doris said, her voice rising in anger.

"But Miss Floretta is out there!" Gail was almost in tears.

"Miss *Who?*" asked Berry.

"Miss Floretta. She lives in my building and she'll tell my parents."

"Quitter, quitter, quitter!" Berry hissed.

"Well, what if somebody who knew your folks was out there?"

"I wouldn't bat an eye," said Berry, "because I smell the money, honey."

"Yeah, me, too," DeeDee chimed in, "I smell the money, honey, and fortune and fame is the name of my game. Besides, I invited my mother, only she had a date with — "

"Listen!" Doris interrupted, grabbing Gail by the shoulders. "This is the opportunity we've been dreaming of, working for! Now, we've come this far — "

Doris stopped in mid-speech at the sound of thunderous applause. The audience was going crazy over the Pickett Sisters.

"Do you hear that?" said Doris, tightening her grip

on Gail's shoulders. "That could be for us. Tonight, next week, and — "

"Halos, you're on," a stagehand called out.

While the emcee introduced The Halos, Doris said a silent prayer: "Dear Lord, I don't think what I'm doing is so wrong, and I don't mean to disobey my mother. But, Lord, you gave me the gift of song and I — " With the adrenaline pumping through her veins and a tornado of emotions raging in her heart, Doris ceased striving to put her feelings into words. As The Halos made their way out onto the stage, Doris simply closed her prayer with the words: "Just guide me, O Thou great Jehovah." Then Doris took two deep breaths and relaxed her shoulders.

During the musical introduction, The Halos broke out into a brisk, coordinated dance step. DeeDee's lipstick was picture perfect. The run in Berry's stockings stayed above her knee. Gail forgot all about Miss Floretta. And as quickly and suddenly as they had swooped in, just as swiftly the butterflies in Doris's stomach swooped out. As The Halos launched into their song, Doris felt an invisible string attached to the top of her head pulling her up to a higher plane.

> *Told me he'd be true,*
> *What am I to do?*
> *He broke into my heart,*
> *Now he's gone.*

> *He said to wait a while,*
> *He'd come back with his smile.*

He broke into my heart,
Now he's gone.

So I waited there,
Each night I said a prayer.
Now I know he's gone,
Gone for Good — ooooooooooooooooo

How can I pretend?
It's over — it's the end.
I'm all alone here
With my song,
And now he's gone.

The Halos were on stage for five minutes; but to them it seemed five seconds. Before they knew it, they were bowing their way offstage to very hearty applause, whistles, and howls.

A few minutes later, all the contestants were lined up onstage. The Halos held their breath every time the emcee placed his hand over the other contestants. When he came to the Pickett Sisters, the audience clapped and clapped. The Halos managed to keep smiles on their faces, but four hearts began to sink. When the emcee finally reached The Halos, four hearts took flight, because the audience clapped and clapped, and kept on clapping.

And then . . . they clapped some more.

As Doris stood there under the brilliance of the lights and the swell of thunderous applause, she was suddenly overcome by that strange sensation people sometimes have while asleep: that flash of awareness that whatever is going on is but a dream.

Doris squeezed her eyes shut and said to herself, "Oh, God, please don't let this be a dream." When she opened her eyes, nothing had changed. There she was onstage, a winner at Amateur Night at the Apollo; and she knew for sure that it was not a dream. And backstage a little while later, when the emcee introduced The Halos to a Miss Ruby Bryant, Doris found out that she had won much more than she had bargained for.

Miss Bryant spoke like the crackerjack business-woman that she was. "Let me just congratulate you all on your performance and your win tonight," Miss Bryant said as she shook each Halo's hand. "I've seen a lot of singers in my time. Some with talent to burn, but no heart. Others who are all heart, but little talent. Now, you girls look like you have a lot of talent and a lot of heart. I'm not saying you couldn't use a little work, but you've definitely got what it takes."

"Why, thank you, ma'am," Doris said.

"Well, I'm just telling it like it is. Over the years I've managed a lot of groups — "

"Oh, I've heard of you," DeeDee interrupted. "You managed the Olympics and — "

"That's right, and a lot more groups that have gone on to make it big-time. And I'm interested in doing the same for you. In no time at all I could have you out on the road."

"When do we leave?" Gail blurted out.

"Not so fast, young lady. First off, you've got to be sure on a gut level that you really want a singing career." As she pulled out some papers from her briefcase, she added, "If the answer is yes, then I want you to look over this contract, and trusting you find everything copacetic, then all you have to do is sign on the dotted line and we'll be in business." As she was about to close her briefcase she asked, "By the way, are any of you under eighteen?"

"Well, we all are," Doris replied.

"In that case," said Miss Bryant as she brought out some more papers, "you'll need to have a parent or legal guardian sign this consent form." She then handed Doris her business card and added, "Feel free to call me if you have any questions, and if I don't hear from you within a week, I'll assume you've all had a change of heart." With that and a handshake, Miss Bryant took her leave.

Doris, Berry, DeeDee, and Gail just stood there and exchanged open-mouthed stares.

"Well, girls," said the emcee, having overheard the conversation, "looks like this has been your lucky night. Ruby Bryant is one of the best in the business, and an offer like this doesn't come every day."

As the emcee moved on, Doris, Berry, DeeDee, and Gail lingered there a while in a daze.

Thirteen

When The Halos reached Seventh Avenue they hugged each other for what must have been by now the hundredth time. When Berry, Gail, and DeeDee got their green light, they proceeded down Seventh Avenue. Doris stood alone on the corner staring at the big red eye that told her, "Stop."

A young man brushed by Doris when the light turned green. He looked back at her over his shoulder, then kept on across the street. By the time he was on the other side of 125th street, Doris was again being told to stop. A minute later the light winked green. Doris knew it was time to go, but she remained rooted in the same spot. Out of the corner of her eye she saw a billy club twirl in the air and heard it slap against flesh.

"Are you lost or something, miss?" inquired the policeman.

"No, sir, I'm on my way home."

The light was again telling Doris she could go, but instead of stepping down from the curb she made an about-face and headed back toward the Apollo. When she reached the Apollo, she kept walking.

The long, steady *bzzzzzzzzz* startled Sister Carrie out of a dream. By the second *bzzzzzzzzz*, she was making her way to the front door and muttering, "Who in the Holy Ghost is ringing my bell this time of night?"

"Who is it?"

"It's me, Sister Carrie. Doris."

"Doris!" Sister Carrie said as she flung open the door.

"Sister Carrie, I need a big favor," said Doris breathlessly, as she whooshed straight into the living room.

"What on earth has happened?"

"Please, Sister Carrie, just sit down and listen."

Poised on the edge of the love seat and without even once interrupting, Sister Carrie listened to Doris's whole tale of The Halos and Amateur Night at the Apollo.

When Doris finished, she felt a tightness in her head and leaned back on the couch. Sister Carrie — legs crossed, elbow on knee, chin in hand — remained silent.

"Sister Carrie . . . now I have to tell Mama, and I'm scared. Could you call home for me and, if she's there, tell her that I'm okay and I'm sleeping over and — "

"Whoa, now, Doris. Just wait one little minute,"

Sister Carrie said, rising slowly and moving over to the window. "I think it's a little late for you to be coming to me about this."

"Please, Sister Carrie. I just need a little time to think. Could you just make something up? Say you needed me to do something or — "

"Doris, don't ask me to lie for you."

There was a long pause. Sister Carrie began to pace. "Doris, how far did you think this through? Did you think about what you win when you win . . . when you follow your dream? Remember, Doris, I've been there."

"Sister Carrie, I — I know what I won. I won Amateur Night at the Apollo. I won a shot at — "

"Doris, I'm not talking about tonight. What I'm talking about is in the long run. Like I said, you got to think about what you win when you win. . . . Doris, are you ready to leave home and be on your own?"

"I think so, Sister Carrie, but . . . could you just come home with me, sort of help me break the news to Mama?"

"You mean help stop her from breaking something over your backside," Sister Carrie snapped. "You say you need time to think. Didn't you do any thinking beforehand?"

During the silence Doris's head began to throb.

"When you thought about winning, you knew your mama would have to find out, right? So, what were you going to do at that point?"

"I, uh, I thought — I don't know, Sister Carrie. All I knew was I had to try to live my dream, give it a start. . . . And I know what you're thinking but, Sister

Carrie, this is not spite-work. I'm not trying to prove anything. I just want to sing."

"Doris, you know I love you with all my heart, but you're going to have to learn how to think and look beyond the next corner. Maybe if you'd told me about this earlier I could've helped you out. But you've already made your bed now."

"But — "

"But what?"

"I — "

"Doris, the only thing I can suggest right now is that you get on home and face the music." Sister Carrie didn't catch the irony of the phrase. She only added, "And the sooner, the better."

Doris sat speechless, just staring at Sister Carrie. Feelings of hurt, betrayal, abandonment gnawed at her heart. Tears were beginning to sting Doris's eyes, but pride and anger told her to keep blinking and fight back the tears. After a long pause Doris rose from the couch and headed from the room.

"Good night, Sister Carrie," she hurled over her shoulder when she reached the front door.

"Wait a minute, Doris," said Sister Carrie as she moved from the living room and down the hall to her bedroom.

Hope came alive in Doris's heart, but it dropped dead when Sister Carrie joined her in the foyer.

"Here, sugar," she said, sticking a dollar bill in Doris's hand. "Get a taxi. When you get outside, stand where I can see you from the window."

Doris left without a word. Not even a "thank you."

After she locked the door, Sister Carrie went to the living room window. As she watched Doris emerge from the building, skitter across the avenue, and, with a slight flick of her wrist and a wave of her hand, make a taxi stop on a dime, she noticed for the first time how graceful Doris had become. She followed the taxi as far as her view would allow, thinking hard about her god-daughter's predicament. With the taxi long out of sight, Sister Carrie leaned her head against the windowpane and sighed. "Doris, it's never going to be the same, chile. It's never going to be the same."

Fourteen

There are not many times in the life of a human being when everything changes in twenty-four hours. You wake up in the morning and everything looks and feels one way. Then, before you go to sleep, nothing is the same. Winning Amateur Night at the Apollo was such a day for Doris Winter. In all the excitement of the dream, Doris had not given any thought to what would be next if the dream became a reality.

Doris walked up the front steps of her house quietly, gingerly, hoping against hope that the Spirit had been so high that her mother was still at Mt. Calvary praising the Lord. Once inside, she found the house dark except for the wall lamp in the front hall that Geraldine always left on when she went out at night.

As Doris began to tiptoe her way upstairs, a light clicked on in the parlor.

Geraldine had fretted herself to exhaustion, and then dozed off in the wing chair by the fireplace. Her mind had been a maze of thoughts of her baby girl attacked in the street and left for dead in some abandoned building, or lying in some hospital unconscious and with broken bones. Naturally, now that she saw that her daughter was home and in one piece, Geraldine was halfway ready to tear Doris apart limb by limb.

"Good evening. Or, rather, good morning, young lady," she said.

"Hi, Mama. How was church?" was all Doris could think to say.

"How was studying?" Geraldine solemnly asked as she beckoned Doris into the parlor.

Once inside the parlor, Doris uttered a mouse-sized, "Fine."

"And I *suppose* this history test is going to be covering the history of the world, from Adam and Eve right on up to the present?"

"It's uh — "

"And I *suppose* that you and Berry were studying so hard that you didn't hear the phone ringing when I called."

"I, uh — "

With each "And I *suppose*," Geraldine leaned forward in her chair, and her voice grew louder. "Doris where have you been?" she asked, rising from the chair.

Doris knew the pause could not last forever. "Singing, Mama. Singing," Doris said softly.

"Doris, I'm going to ask you one more time! Where in the world have you been!"

"The . . . Apollo," Doris stammered.

"Excuse me?"

"I was at the . . . Apollo," she repeated, her chin almost to her chest.

"The *Apollo*? The *Apollo*?"

"Tonight was Amateur Night at the Apollo," Doris interrupted. As she did, she slowly raised her head. "I started a group, Mama. The Halos. And The Halos and I — "

"You been *singing* at the *Apollo*?"

"Yes, Mama."

"The *APOLLO*?

"But, Mama, Amateur Night at the Apollo is where you get discovered. It's where a lot of big-time singers got their start."

"Got their start at what? Big-time drinking? Big-time drugs? Big-time getting beat up, cut up, and run down?"

"Got their start on recordings, singing in front of thousands of people, seeing the world."

Geraldine stood speechless.

"Mama, we won tonight. The Halos won Amateur Night at the Apollo. Mama, I'm sorry I lied to you, but this was such an opportunity to — and, Mama, we won. The Halos won. Do you understand what that means?"

Geraldine just stood there in disbelief.

"We get to perform again at the Apollo. But, Mama, not only that! Miss Ruby Bryant, who's managed a lot of singers, came up to us backstage and said we got what it takes and, Mama, she's interested in managing us and taking us out on the road. But

I need your permission. I need you to sign a consent form. This paper right here, Mama."

"The only place you're going is up to your room and stay there until I decide what I'm going to do about you and your Halos and coming home from the Apollo at this time of morning, without a telephone call, a word, or nothing. Amateur Night, huh! Yeah, Doris Winter, you sure are some amateur."

"But, Mama — "

"But Mama nothing! *MOVE!*" Geraldine shouted, raising her arm and pointing Doris out of the parlor and up the stairs.

After Doris scurried out, Geraldine began to pace the parlor floor and unleash her wrath on the empty room. "Seventeen years old, coming in here at one o'clock in the morning! She's got a contract! She's going out on the road! No, no, no, you don't! Not as long as you living under *my* roof! Eating *my* food! Wearing the clothes *I* put on your back!"

Geraldine stormed out to the front hall and shouted up to the top of the stairs, " 'Round here acting like you grown! Going out on the road! Oh, no, baby girl. Oh, no! I am your mother and you are my child. Seventeen years ago I brought you *into* this world and I can — "

Geraldine stopped herself from saying "And I can take you out!" She had always cringed when she heard a mother bash a child with those words, a mother who in a fit of anger and frustration dared to say she would play God. And on the day all seven pounds and eight ounces of Doris came into this world, hadn't Geraldine looked down at her baby girl and vowed to cherish her always as a gift from God?

Geraldine returned to the parlor and slumped into the wing chair. She tilted her head up and closed her eyes. When she opened them, she saw Doris standing in the doorway.

Doris was still dressed as she was when she came home. But now she had her overnight bag in one hand, her Pullman suitcase in the other.

Geraldine leaned forward in the chair. Then she fell back limp. She cocked her head to the side and sighed. "Rev . . . looks like I've done something wrong somewhere along the line." Geraldine looked at Doris long and hard. Then she let fly the last weapon she had. "Doris, what on earth, chile, what on earth do you think your father would have to say if he could see you now?"

Before Doris knew it, the words were flowing. "Mama, the night before Daddy died, he told me to follow my dream. Going out on the road with The Halos is following my dream. Becoming a singer, Mama, is my dream. Mama, I want to sing. . . . I want to sing. And, Mama, I want your blessing, but, Mama, if you don't sign the consent form — "

Doris broke off, dropped her suitcases, stepped slowly into the parlor, and moved toward her mother. Then she held out the consent form. Geraldine stared down at it, then up at Doris, then back down. Doris laid the consent form on the table next to her mother's chair, sat down on the piano bench, and stared out the window.

Doris tried several times to finish her sentence. The words, "Mama, if you don't sign, I'm leaving,

I'm going," raced through her head, but her heart was keeping her mouth shut. Why did she have to choose? Her mother over The Halos. Her mother over song. Her mother and everything she knew over going out on the road and following her dream.

Doris looked out into the black night for a star. The next thing she knew, the chorus of a song she hadn't sung for years was running through her mind:

> *I sing because I'm happy,*
> *I sing because I'm free,*
> *For His eye is on the sparrow,*
> *And I know He watches me.*

Doris wanted to look at her mother. She wanted to see her eyes, to read them. But Doris was afraid. So instead, she continued to stare out the window, unable to shake the song from her mind.

The doorbell pierced their distance. Doris and Geraldine turned to one another with the same puzzled look in their eyes. Doris moved to get up, but when Geraldine said, "I'll get it," she quickly slumped back down.

When the front door opened, Doris heard, "Figured you'd be up. And I also figured all hell might be breaking loose 'bout now. 'Scuse my language, but it's hard to be totally righteous this time of morning."

When Sister Carrie entered the parlor, Doris avoided her eyes. Sister Carrie sat down on the couch. Geraldine returned to the wing chair.

"Did you tell your mama you stopped by me tonight?"

"No."

Geraldine shot Doris a look that asked, And what else don't I know about?

"Geraldine, she told me everything and I told her to go on home and talk to you."

"So she came to you first?"

"Geraldine, the girl was scared out of her wits! . . . Anyway, after she left, I got to thinking and — Doris would you excuse us, please?"

Doris left the room without a word.

In her mind's eye, Sister Carrie followed Doris upstairs. When she heard her footsteps cross the threshold of her bedroom, she turned to Geraldine and saw tears streaming down her face. Sister Carrie took a handkerchief from her purse and went over and handed it to her best friend.

"Geraldine," she said softly, "Geraldine, you know there comes a time in every mother's life when she's got to let her child go — "

"Carrie, I don't want to hear that."

"Now, Geraldine," she said tenderly but firmly. "This is Sister Carrie speaking. I believe the Lord allows certain people to remain in our lives just to remind us of where he has brought us from. I remember a time not so long ago when your mama had a T-I-M-E with you. There was this young handsome Bajan minister with only one suit and two good shirts, but he had a dream . . . and a vision. And soon that dream became yours, too. Things didn't work out so bad, now, did they?"

Sister Carrie returned to the couch and reached into her purse for a piece of peppermint candy. She held one out to Geraldine. Geraldine took the piece of candy and slowly removed the wrapper. She put the candy in her mouth and with her tongue tossed it from cheek to cheek.

When Sister Carrie felt the pause had lasted long enough, she smiled and slowly began to move toward Geraldine. "Sit up and be strong, Geraldine. And remember the words of Proverbs, chapter twenty-two, verse six: 'Train up a child in the way he should go: and when he is old, he will not depart from it.' "

Geraldine looked up at Sister Carrie, trying to draw on her strength. "But she's so young, Carrie. She's so young. How can — " Geraldine broke off, dropped her head in her hands, and burst into tears.

"I know, Geraldine, I know," Sister Carrie said as she moved behind the wing chair. She rested her hands on Geraldine's shoulders and added, "But, Geraldine, Doris has a dream and vision all her own. Let her go, Geraldine. You can't hold her. Nobody can force nobody forever. Somehow, I believe she won't lose her way. Geraldine, I want you to sit here and think about what I've said. And if you don't mind, I'd like to have a few words with Doris."

"Talk to her Carrie. Let her know what's going on," Geraldine pleaded between her tears.

Upstairs, Doris was lying facedown on her bed, mulling over her plan of action for the tenth time. First thing tomorrow morning I'm leaving, she thought to herself. She's not gonna keep her foot on my neck for the rest of my life! If Toni's parents won't let me stay with them, I'm sure DeeDee's mother will understand. I'll tell Miss Bryant my mother spilled coffee on the consent form and get

another one from her, and I'll forge her signature. I
don't need her, I can —

" "May I come in?" Sister Carrie said with three
quick raps on Doris's bedroom door.

"Uh-huh," Doris said with a sniffle.

"Hey, there, sugar plum," Sister Carrie said, drop-
ping Doris's suitcases near the dresser.

Doris ran into Sister Carrie's arms and held on to
her with all her might.

"There, there, sugar. There, there." As she led
Doris over to the bed she added, "Everything's
gonna be all right."

Sister Carrie rocked Doris for a long while.

"Sugar plum, now I don't want to jump the gun,
but if I were you, I'd stop fretting for the time being.
And I want you to listen to me and listen good."

"Yes, Sister Carrie, . . . I'm listening."

"Success is no trick. It's a lot more than talent
and it's a lot more than hard work. The key word is
balance, in both your work and your fun. And when
it comes to the last one, the best way I can put it
is this: You've got to know when to leave the party."

"Know when to leave the party?"

"What I'm saying is, if you decide to go through
with following your dream, you're going to find all
kinds of temptations coming at you left and right.
Sometimes, what's wrong is gonna seem so right
and what's right is gonna seem strange, not to mention boring. So you got to always keep in touch with
yourself, check yourself, and make sure you know
when to leave the party. Remember who you are,
remember your home training, and remember where

you came from. Be sweet, be kind, be humble, and be *careful*."

"Know when to leave the party," Doris said with a nod. "I think I understand what you're trying to tell me. I'll take care of myself. I won't forget who I am."

"Promise?"

"Promise."

Again Sister Carrie and Doris hugged. Each with all her might.

"Now, I want you to get in bed and rest yourself," Sister Carrie said. "Do some thinking, but don't think too hard. I'll tell your mama that you're as snug as a bug in a rug."

"Thank you, Sister Carrie. . . . I love you."

"I love you, too, sugar plum."

After Sister Carrie left, Doris changed into her nightclothes. As she lay in bed she felt cozy inside. She didn't overthink. She didn't underthink. She just "was." And soon, she was asleep.

The next morning Doris woke up with confusion. She felt weak and decided that if she were going to run away, she'd wait until after breakfast. As she was dressing, there was a knock at her door.

"Come in."

"Good morning, Doris."

"Good morning, Mama."

Geraldine sat at Doris's desk. Doris slunk to her bed and sat down facing her mother.

After a long pause Geraldine asked, "When's your last day of school?"

"June twenty-third."

"I see." After another pause she asked, "And there won't be any problem with your graduating? I mean, you haven't let your schoolwork slide with all this, this, uh — "

"Oh, no, Mama. And I think I'll actually do pretty well. *B*'s. Except maybe not in history."

At the word "history," both mother and daughter cleared their throats.

"I see," said Geraldine, finally breaking the silence and the tension. "I see." After another pause she continued. "This Miss, er, um, Miss — " As she searched for the name, she pulled the consent form from her apron pocket. "Miss Bryant," she said finally, once again scanning the piece of paper she had by now read over a hundred times.

"She's managed a lot of singing groups," Doris offered "She discovered the Regals, the Olympics, the — "

"Doris."

"Yes, Mama?"

"I'm going to call this Miss Bryant within the next few hours. Going to see if I can get an appointment with her sometime between today and tomorrow. I want to see her face. Look into her eyes. And if I believe she's gonna do what she says she's gonna do. . . . If . . . "

May 1, 1952

Dear Diary,

  Mama's "If" became a "Yes!" I'm gonna sing. I'm gonna sing!

That next week Geraldine and Sister Carrie were in the front row of the Apollo every night. Sister Carrie kept saying to herself, I better not hear a peep out of the Mt. Calvary busybody committee about my godchild. And Geraldine had that I'm-so-proud-of-my-baby smile on her face.

Then, that summer, after they graduated from high school, The Halos went out on the road. For many years they sang in small cities and large ones, searching for that one big break — that one hit record that would take them to the top of the charts. There were long bus rides, short romances, and one or two promoters who ran away with their money. The Halos got down but they never gave up. With each gig, with each record, their popularity grew, and success came closer within their reach. And one day they had a nice little piece of it in their hands.

Doris remained the driving force behind the group, and its brightest star, so that it wasn't long before the group was known as "Doris Winter and the Halos." As time rolled on, Berry came down with the common celebrity syndrome: swollen-head-itis. She decided she could only make it really big-time if she went solo with her career. She left the group and soloed her way into obscurity. Gail never learned when to leave the party: she ran herself ragged and into an early grave. And to everyone's surprise, DeeDee fell in love with a chubby, unassuming house painter from Brooklyn, and a husband and children became the name of her game.

Doris's spirit didn't move too well with any of the

replacement Halos. Soon The Halos were no more.
And Doris Winter pressed on alone.

One day, in a flash of inspiration, Doris booked
a studio and, in one take, wrote the song that
catapulted her into international stardom. The year
was 1963; the song, "Just One Look." The song was
eventually recorded by eighty different singing
groups in ten different countries.

Over the years, Doris was rewarded for her talent
and hard work: six gold records, four platinum albums, three Grammy awards.

Through it all, Doris never lost her joy.

Epilogue

Doris Winter was fighting back tears as the ushers took up offering on that windy autumn Sunday morning. When Geraldine, seated on her left, dropped a twenty-dollar bill in the plate, Doris cocked her head to the side and let out a little chuckle. Sister Carrie, on her right in a hot-pink suit and matching suede pumps with half-inch heels, nudged Doris and tucked a piece of peppermint candy into her hand.

The text for Reverend Grady's sermon that day was Proverbs, chapter 3, verses 5 and 6:

> TRUST IN THE LORD WITH ALL THINE HEART; AND LEAN NOT UNTO THY OWN UNDERSTANDING. IN ALL THY WAYS ACKNOWLEDGE HIM, AND HE SHALL DIRECT THY PATHS.

As Reverend Grady brought his sermon to a close, Doris thought, I guess my time is near. After the altar

call, Reverend Grady cleared his throat and his face
lit up.

"As you all know, there's a little different order
to our service today. Before we close out, we're
going to hear a few words from one of our church
daughters, our guest speaker for the day, Miss — "

The congregation broke out into fierce applause.
Doris tried to fight back the tears welling up in her
eyes, but she lost. The tears won.

The applause continued. The entire congregation
was on its feet. Reverend Grady tried to quiet them
down, but soon gave up. He looked out at Doris
and shouted over the applause, "Doris, I tried to
give you a proper introduction, but looks like I can't
do nothing with them, so you might as well come
on up here."

Doris had been standing in the pulpit for four
minutes before the congregation finally settled
down. So many of the great African American singers of her generation had learned to sing in a church
choir. Now it was time to say "thank you."

"Mt. Calvary provided me with so much," Doris
Winter said. "So much music, so much energy, so
much knowledge, and so much love. It was here,
so many years ago, that I learned how to sing, how
to feel, how to think, how to allow the Spirit to move
through me."

The audience and the congregation sat in a
hushed silence.

"And, as you can see, the Spirit is moving through
me right now." The Minister of Music brought a
tissue for her to dry her eyes.

"Dear hearts," Doris continued, "I am pleased to

announce this morning that I have purchased and
renovated a brownstone on 126th Street. And tomorrow a school will open in that building. A school
for musically gifted children, ages twelve through
sixteen." Extending her hand toward her mother,
Doris added, "The school will bear the name 'The
Geraldine Winter School for Gifted Children.' "

A burst of applause filled Mt. Calvary.

"And, finally, I just want to say thank you. Thank
you, choir. Thank you, Brother Wesley. Thank you,
Sister Carrie. Thank you, Mama." Tilting her head
up slightly she added, "And thank you, Daddy." After
a tearful pause she closed with, "Thank you all. I
love you. You will never be far from my heart."

It would be another three hours before Doris
would leave Mt. Calvary. Everybody wanted an autograph, a word, a smile, a hug. And she couldn't
say no to a quick lunch downstairs in the cafeteria.

When Doris descended the steps of Mt. Calvary
Full Gospel Church, the sun was nowhere to be
found, but a band of its amber rays still glowed in
the deep dark azure sky. With her driver in position
beside the open car door, Doris helped Geraldine
and Sister Carrie in and then turned toward the
church and blew kisses to the crowd. As the limousine pulled away from the curb, Doris gave Mt.
Calvary a parting glance and thought, Yes, I have
come this far by faith. The faith on which Mt. Calvary
was built, my father's faith in divine guidance, and
in the end, Mama's faith in me.

About the Authors

VY HIGGINSEN and her husband Ken Wydro wrote, produced, and directed the musical *Mama, I Want to Sing*, and its sequel. The musical was inspired by Ms. Higginsen's sister Doris Troy, a composer and singer in the 1960s. Higginsen has worked in a range of fields, from fashion buyer to television talk show host. She lives in New York with her husband and daughter, Knoelle.

Although this is her first novel, TONYA BOLDEN is an experienced writer and researcher. The author of *The Family Heirloom Cookbook*, she has also written numerous articles and literary reviews that have appeared in magazines and newspapers including *The New York Times Book Review*, *Essence*, and *The Amsterdam News*. She lives in New York City.